PRAISE FOR JOHN LYNCH

John Lynch's Expiration of Sentence is a brutal, unflinching tale of pure, adrenaline-filled horror.

DUNCAN RALSTON — AUTHOR OF PEDO ISLAND BLOODBATH

EXPIRATION OF SENTENCE

JOHN LYNCH

JOHN LYNCH
HIGH EXPLOSIVE HORROR

For Britney, El, William and Ronan

CHAPTER ONE

"Mr. Murphy, you sit here before the parole board today and present yourself well. You've taken every class recommended to you, volunteer in the mentorship program, and aside from a few scattered incidents here and there, your discipline record within the institution paints you in a favorable light," said Mr. Doyle.

"Thank you, Mr. Doyle. I understand I can't change what I've done, but I know that every day I have a new opportunity to put my best foot forward and work on becoming a better me. Each day is one day closer to going home, and I think I am ready to reintegrate into society. I'm glad that..."

Sean Doyle cleared his throat, cutting off inmate Richard Murphy, identification number 115374, mid speech. "Mr. Murphy, please, I'm not finished speaking. Before you count your chickens, maybe you should listen to *everything* the board has to say."

Murphy swallowed what felt like a meatball sized lump. His prison jumper was soaked in sweat despite the meat locker like chill in the room. His heart felt as if it had sunk deep into the pit of his stomach. He'd been hopeful, but he was no dummy and he could already tell which direction this conversation was headed. It was a done deal, the board members' minds made up. He tuned Doyle out. There was no need to listen to the fucking toolbag lecture him. Listen to him take a shit on his hopes and dreams. Whatever the man said to him was nothing more than a long winded, roundabout way of saying two words.

Parole Denied.

Even with the outcome a forgone conclusion, he couldn't just get up and walk away, he had to stick around and let this asshole talk down to him and take it like a bitch. If he were to behave in any other manner, they'd have it out for him again the next time parole consideration came around. Murphy learned long ago that while in prison, the easiest way to do your bid was to avoid making waves. Whether good or bad, leaving an impression on someone rarely led to anything good around here.

Doyle continued. "As I was going to say, you *present well.* But I know that you're a smart man, Mr. Murphy. You aren't like many of the other inmates around here. You admit what you've done. You appear to show remorse for your crime. But you'll notice the key word there. You *appear* to show remorse, Mr. Murphy. I believe that a smart man such as yourself is simply playing the game. You aren't remorseful for your crime. You killed a man. And not only did you kill another human being, but you plotted and schemed with meticulous detail what you were going to do and when you were going to do it. And what you did to that man, regardless of the crime that *he* committed against your family, takes an especially twisted mind to carry out. This was no heat of the moment situation, were that the case special consideration may be granted. But Mr. Murphy, when I look into your eyes, I see a man who, if given the ability to go back in time and change his actions, he would instead choose to behave the same way. And enjoy doing so."

Murphy slammed his fists on the table, shaking the large

rectangular piece of furniture. Doyle looked as if he shit his pants, surprised at the outburst. Who knows, maybe he did. Suits like him talked tough, but at the slightest sign of trouble, the bitch in them appeared.

"You're right," Murphy said. "I would do it again. That scumbag molested my son. He did it multiple times. My son's life is ruined because of that fucking monster. And what did the state do? What did they consider *justice*?"

The two officers stationed in the room approached Murphy in case things spun out of control, but let him keep speaking. Everyone knew what he was in for. Most of the correction officers would have done the same thing if placed in his shoes and readily admit as much.

"The judge gave that piece of shit a light sentence on a plea deal. Five years to serve with 15 years suspended. And you all on this very board let that fucking scumbag out two years early for good behavior? He raped a fucking child and served *three fucking years*. There are guys doing more time in here for selling weed. Guys in here doing more time for bull-shit theft charges, yet diddlers get soft sentences and parole for good behavior when what they really deserve is to be dragged out back and shot, for the good of society. Every single one of you should be ashamed of yourselves. I did what the state would have done if our lawmakers had a set of balls between them."

The room was silent. After a moment Doyle started to speak, but Murphy had heard enough. If they remembered this outburst the next go around, so be it. He'd serve the full sentence if that's what it took. Murphy didn't have to go to bed at night knowing some scumbag he let out early might rape another kid, but these boards members would. The man he'd murdered had hardly been the first piece of shit they let out, and he sure as shit wouldn't be the last, either.

Hands gripping the edge of the table, he pushed himself up from the chair. The two officers monitoring the hearing reached for their cuffs and pepper spray but didn't immediately react. Murphy shook his head. "I'm all set, guys," he said to the officers. "You're not gonna have any problems with me. I'm just done with this bullshit hearing. I'll go back to my cell now."

He strolled out of the room calmly, although he felt anything *but*. His blood boiled in his veins, and he felt ready to snap at the slightest provocation. The rage simmered underneath the surface. The last time that happened, Murphy had killed a man. That was the real reason he excused himself from the parole meeting. Not because of the mic drop he'd just performed on the parole board, but because in his mind he pictured himself hopping across the table and choking the life out of Doyle. Squeezing his neck until his beady little eyes popped out of his fucking skull like the scumbag he was. He saw himself pounding the man's face over and over until it was broken and battered. Teeth shattered, eyes swollen shut. Nose twisted and mangled. Being carried away in handcuffs while Doyle's face lay bleeding, looking like raw ground beef. Images that had flashed before his eyes in a few brief moments.

He smiled, thinking about the visions. He liked what he saw.

But a cooler head prevailed. Murphy knew it better to leave the room on his own accord, lest he end up facing an assault charge, possibly even an attempted murder. The threat of new assault charges was not one Murphy took lightly, but the thought of being pepper sprayed and dragged out of the hearing in handcuffs by the two meathead officers in the room was even more of a deterrent.

Murphy was alone in his cell. He'd stuffed a towel in the narrow window frame, blocking sunlight from getting through. The environment matched his mood, and he was ok with that. Sometimes he liked the dark, felt at home in it. It would be some time before his cellmate, Lewis, returned. He was enrolled in community college classes in the education area and wouldn't be back for at least another hour, possibly two. Murphy was thankful for the alone time. He wanted to stew in his thoughts, unbothered. Physically, he ran through his daily cell workout routine as if he'd never had a hearing to begin with—business as usual. But mentally, his mind raced as numerous scenarios and what-ifs swirled about his mind. Parole was out of the question.

Not only had he been denied, but after his outburst he'd been given a two-year review, rather than the standard one. A big fuck you to Murphy for speaking his mind. And two years from now when he was up for review again? Well, common sense told him it would be nothing more than a formality. He'd blown any chance of the parole board *not* having a poor impression of him at the next meeting. It was never a smart move to piss in the Cheerios of those who had the fate of your future in their hands, and he'd done just that. If he was lucky, maybe there would be new parole board members at the next hearing. At least that way it would be like having a fresh start. A new chance to show everyone how *rehabilitated* he was.

All roads led to one conclusion: there was no chance in hell he would be leaving Glenwood Correctional Institute in the near future.

Murphy paced back and forth in his cell in between sets of his workout—push-ups, body weight squats, jumping jacks, and sit-ups. Those forty-five seconds were supposed to be a respite from the intense workout he put himself through, and while it allowed his body a moment to breathe, those few moments of rest were when his mind ran rampant. He completed fifteen sets of his circuit, five more than usual. After completing the circuit, exhaustion took over, and he collapsed on his bunk, too tired to change or shower.

Murphy slept like the dead, only stirring from his sleep when the area officer kicked his door during his nightly count.

CHAPTER TWO

Murphy awoke the next morning to the sound of watery shit splattering in the toilet. The stench of human feces threatened to choke Murphy in the confines of the small cell. He gagged and struggled to not vomit.

"Man, what the fuck?" Murphy said to his cellmate, Darius Lewis.

Lewis laughed. "My bad, man," he said, "you know those spicy chicken patties they give us in the chow hall give me the bubble guts."

"You call that bubble guts? It smells like something died in your ass, resurrected, and died again. That's fucking putrid."

"I've got IBS, asshole, I told you that. Now you can either deal with me shitting myself every so often, or I can let the C.O. know that you're watching me shit. You know they take that prison rape shit serious now. I bet you'll get a week in segregation if I tell them you were scoping out my hang down."

"It's not that serious man, besides you know I left my elec-tron microscope at home. I couldn't see your baby dick if I tried. And not for nothing, the feds give a shit about the prison rape elimination act, but this place has gotten far worse since I've been here, and I don't think anyone gives a flying fuck what we do here as long as we do it quietly."

"You want to find out? Maybe we will get single cells out of it, at least until the next new commit comes in and that shiny, empty bunk gets an occupant. So, you can deal with bubble guts, or I can tell the officer you're making sexual comments to me. Who knows, maybe when you get out of seg, the next guy they stick you with will be some nasty fuck that doesn't shower. Or a thief. Or some fucking sex fiend. Or…"

"Lewis, I get it. You're the best cell mate I'm ever gonna have. Please, just wipe your ass man, I need to call my wife and tell her the bad news."

Lewis finished wiping his ass, flushed the toilet, and washed his hands. He shook his head in disbelief at the revelation that Murphy had yet to tell his wife the bad news. "Bro, you better call that woman. She's gonna fuck you up if she hears from someone else that they denied your parole. You should have told her that last night."

"Yeah, I know. I just didn't know how to break it to her. I'm gonna go eat breakfast when they call chow. Give myself some time to figure out how to break it to her. I'll give her the bad news on a full stomach."

Murphy sat on the metal stool at the far end of one of the dining tables in the mess hall. The tables and stools were uncomfortable, unforgiving. Bolted to the ground, they were nothing more than solid, unmovable pieces of steel. Most things that were large and heavy enough to be used as either weapons or escape tools were bolted down or kept locked behind cages.

The overpowering smell of onions wafted through the mess hall. For whatever reason, onions were used in damn near every meal and the disgusting funk of them spilled out of the exhaust vents in the kitchen's roof, but that didn't stop the aroma from making its way into the dining room and assaulting the olfactory senses of every person in the area. It was disgusting. Murphy couldn't stand onions. Who the fuck would think it was a good idea to use them in so many recipes? It had to be some kind of cruel prank on the inmates.

There were plenty of inmates who'd love to work in the kitchen. It was a position that came with the luxury of being away from the general population most of the day, preparing your own food, and eating plenty of meals the rest of the inmates didn't get. But the tradeoff was that the stench of the kitchen seeped into your clothes and skin. The result was a funk that followed you wherever you went, no matter how clean you were. Murphy didn't think the pros outweighed the cons, so he never bothered requesting a job in the kitchen or the dining room.

He shoveled runny scrambled eggs into his mouth, washing the slop down with a carton of milk that was set to expire today. Best not to dwell on whether or not the chunks laboring down his throat were from the food or the milk. *Nothing but the best for us.* Murphy didn't bother with the hard slab of charred bread they had the balls to call toast. The hunk of bread was hard enough to break a window, but even if it *weren't* burned to a crisp, the assholes in charge of the menu didn't even bother serving it with the usual slab of butter. Who the hell eats dry toast? Either the kitchen stock was running low, or someone had pissed off one of these officers this morning—likely his wife—and he decided to take it out on the inmates.

Though he believed it should have been impossible,

somehow over the years he'd been locked up, the food had gotten worse. Not that it was ever *good*, but there used to be the occasional decent meal. Prisons weren't known for the quality of their cuisine, but Jesus Christ, the food should at least be edible. Things could be worse, though. If the inmates who'd done time in southern states were to be believed, there were some real horror story meals out there. Prisons where the entire menu comprised nothing but low-quality deli meat sandwiches and hard-boiled eggs.

Maybe I shouldn't complain about the food.

With most of the edible parts of his meal finished and the garbage left untouched, Murphy reached across his tray to grab the one thing he'd actually been looking forward to eating: the blueberry cake. It was nothing special, but the cake was usually moist, and the blueberries had real flavor. He considered this pastry the one *good* item on the current rotating menu, and had it not been included in this morning's breakfast he likely would have remained in his housing area and waited until the horrid stench of Lewis' ass dissipated before throwing a breakfast together out of his commissary purchases.

As his fingers gripped the cake, lifting it from the tray, a large, tattooed hand closed over his, squeezing the bones together.

Murphy's heart pounded, threatening to burst from his rib cage as adrenaline spiked through his system. A situation like the one he found himself in was undesirable in a correctional institution, but he recognized the tattoo adorning the massive bear paw enveloping his own hand and knew *undesirable* was an understatement.

The hand belonged to Jason Reese, the 'heavy' of the housing block Murphy lived in, and the piece of shit leader of Glenwood's white supremacist gang.

Reese wrenched Murphy's wrist, flipped his hand over

and snatched the blueberry cake from Murphy's grasp. "You weren't gonna eat this, were you?" Reese asked.

"Nah, you can have it, man."

"Yeah, I know I can. But I want to make sure *you* know I can."

"Must be nice to have juice like that around here."

"It *is* nice, having whatever you want. *You* can have whatever you want, too. You just gotta stop being a race traitor and pick a side."

"Pick a side? What side? I'm on *my* side. I want to do my bid and get out."

"Do you remember we just established I get what the fuck I want? I'm giving you some leeway here because we respect what you did to that piece of shit that fucked with your kid. That's the type of motherfucker I want to roll with. I'm guiding you to the right decision, just in case you're too fucking stupid to make it on your own. You know, lead a horse to water and shit. In this scenario, you're the horse, so take the fucking drink." Reese paused for dramatic effect before continuing.

"So when you leave this dining room, you're gonna walk back to the block and you're not even gonna go to your cell. You're gonna stop right at the officer's desk and tell him you don't want to live with anyone but whites from here on out. You're done hanging with anyone who doesn't look like us, you understand? I don't ask twice, so believe me when I tell you this is as far as my grace extends. Like I said before, I respect what you did, but I'll be more than happy to make you my bitch if you keep acting like one."

Pontification over, Reese took a mouthful of Murphy's blueberry cake and then tossed the rest at Murphy's chest. Murphy said nothing in response, sat in silence and watched as Reese stood, brushed his hands on the front of his jumper. He pulled at the bottom of the shirt, straightening the wrinkles in the orange uniform before sticking his chest out and strutting from the mess hall. Reese always made it a point to peacock anytime he entered or exited a room. He was the baddest man in the entire prison, and although everyone from inmate to officer knew it, Reese still liked to bring extra attention to himself any time he could.

As Murphy watched Reese leave, Ralph Adams, the disgusting excuse for a human that sat diagonally across from Murphy, in the seat next to where Reese had sat, cleared his throat and asked, "You gonna eat that, buddy? I'm still hungry." Before Murphy could respond, he reached his filthy hands—stained with years of grime—across the table and snatched the remnants of cake from Murphy's tray. As he brought the blueberry cake to his mouth, crumbs of cake sprinkling from between his disgusting digits, another skinhead came up behind Adams, whispered something in his ear, and stuck a blade in the man's back. Adam's body went rigid. The food crumbs mixed with blood dribbled from between his lips. He coughed, spraying the mixture across the table. Dotting Murphy and the inmate next to him with little crimson droplets. The skinhead locked eyes with Murphy and winked at him as if to say 'see, nobody fucks with one of us' before dropping the shank to the ground and placing his hands on his head, signifying to responding officers he was compliant, no longer a threat.

Murphy shook his head and remained seated until officers cleared the area so nursing staff could perform life-saving measures on Adams until the rescue arrived. If the man was lucky, he'd pull through.

Murphy didn't care either way, Adams was no friend of his.

He left the scene of the attack as instructed.

It was far too early in the morning to deal with this much fucking *excitement*, and Murphy still needed to break the bad news to his wife.

Today was going to be a long day.

CHAPTER THREE

The call wasn't going well, which was exactly as Murphy had expected. His wife continued assaulting his ear, "I had to hear from my goddamn mother-in-law that you didn't make parole! How the fuck do you think that felt? At no point did it occur to you that maybe you should pick the phone up and call your fucking wife? Maybe let her know you *weren't* coming home? I waited around all day for you to call me, but no, you couldn't be bothered. That would have been the considerate thing to do. But Richard fucking Murphy doesn't give a shit about what's going on in anyone's head but his own. Instead, Marge called me this morning to tell me she spoke with your counselor, and they told her they denied you parole. You're a piece of shit, you know that?"

Murphy sighed. He listened to his wife berate him, offered no defense. What else could he do? She had a point. He twirled a pen around in his hand as he watched the inmates go about their business throughout the cell block. It was a habit of his to divide his attention between phone calls and his surroundings. Call it paranoia, or call it survival instincts, but when you're locked up and surrounded by razor wire, you never knew when someone might try you. Weakness was picked out much the same way a shark detected blood. Prey didn't last long behind bars.

The very first day he'd arrived in the block after his sentencing he'd witnessed a man smash another inmates head in with the phone, beating the man repeatedly with the handset until his face looked like raw hamburger. The handset was heavy duty to prevent it from being easily broken, which also meant it could do some real damage. When the handset eventually shattered, the attacking man wrapped the cord around his victim's neck and strangled him with it until correctional staff responded with batons and pepper spray. The attacker spent thirty days in segregation while the man who'd been brutally beaten spent three weeks at Glenwood Memorial Hospital. The beating was so bad the inmate had lost sight in his left eye.

Glenwood Correctional Institute had never been the safest prison. In fact, the original facility had burned to rubble years ago, the result of years of turmoil ending in a catastrophic riot. Things took a severe downward turn immediately following the hire of a new, mysterious warden—a man that to this day is as much of an enigma as he was back then— after the previous warden turned up dead under questionable circumstances. Many of the senior officers were terminated following the warden's arrival and were replaced with new officers who had little to no experience in corrections. The termination of the senior staff members meant there was nobody around to teach the new guys the ropes, but what the new hires lacked in experience, they made up for with a willingness to put hands on inmates at any given time. Violence spiked across the board. Inmate on inmate, inmate on staff, and staff on inmate violence reached all-time highs until the place had gotten so bad the state kept an ambulance on standby in the parking lot.

The states financial woes, along with local political issues, meant that the situation went ignored and unchecked until it was far too gone to *right the ship*. When it was all said and done and the fingerprinting and blame placing ceased, the one thing everyone had agreed on was that Glenwood Correctional Institute was an 'evil' place.

But a necessary evil.

While the facility had been reduced to rubble, there was still a need to house members of the population who couldn't conform to the laws of society—Glenwood Correctional Institute had been rebuilt in record time, but the state's fiscal responsibility to the taxpayers meant drastic measures were taken to complete the project with a minimal budget within a record amount of time. There simply was nowhere to house the inmates, so the state made agreements with neighboring states to temporarily house the displaced inmates during construction of the new facility. The cost-cutting measures included the consolidation of the prison's satellite buildings into the new facility, and the reclassification of inmates to lower security status designations they had no business being classified as.

If that weren't bad enough, Glenwood's already decimated staffing levels mixed with the inability of law enforcement agencies nationwide to properly recruit and hire new staff meant that Glenwood, a department that low staff levels had always plagued, now approached crisis level. In prior years, recruitment classes previously numbered in the hundreds, but were now reduced to dozens. To combat this, issues that would have been grounds for disqualification from the hiring process were now overlooked in order to bolster the ranks. Corrupt officers were no longer slipping through the cracks, they were invited with open arms.

All of that meant one thing for Murphy—if the simple fact of being incarcerated meant he must always remain vigilant, then the deplorable state of GCI increased the need for vigilance tenfold.

"Are you there? Hello?" his wife asked.

Murphy snapped back to reality. Lost in his thoughts, he hadn't heard a word his wife said. "Yeah. Yeah, I'm here. I was just thinking."

"I need you. You need to appeal this decision, or something. Your son needs his father." A click on the other end of the line.

Murphy slammed the handset onto the cradle over and over until the earpiece broke off. He dropped the phone and let it hang, swinging back and forth like a pendulum.

Someone grabbed him by the shoulder. "Hey man, what the fuck did you break the phone for?"

After the morning he had, Murphy was a ticking time bomb and the intrusion into his personal space lit his short fuse. He turned around, swinging his fist wildly as he pivoted. A perfectly placed punch, Murphy's knuckles connected with the man's jaw, smashing his teeth together with an audible click. The skinhead dropped to the floor like a sack of shit.

One of Reese's henchmen, Spencer.

Seeing red and unable to control himself, Murphy jumped on top of Spencer. It didn't matter that the man was already out cold. Murphy pounded him, raining blows from above, pummeling the man's defenseless face and body. Blood and spit flew from his mouth. His nose pancaked and twisted with a sickening crunch. Each strike bounced Spencer's head off the ground like a basketball.

The beating continued until Lewis rushed in and wrapped his arms around Murphy, doing his best to calm the man down and keep him off of Spencer. Eventually, responding officers rushed into the housing unit, batons and pepper spray at the ready.

"Everyone take a fucking knee, nobody move!" One officer shouted.

Murphy was already face down with his hands over his

head. He wanted no part of the department's fight response, but it didn't matter because these were the new breed of officer, the ones who were going to take their pound of flesh when called upon, regardless of if force was still necessary by the time they arrived on the scene. Murphy gave no resistance and complied with the orders being shouted to him, but the moment he heard an officer scream, "Stop resisting," he knew he was fucked.

Almost immediately after someone had screamed the words, a baton found its home across his shoulder blades with a loud, meaty thump. Even as the baton bruised his flesh, he heard the unmistakable *whoosh* of a trigger-happy officer painting his face orange with a can of pepper spray the size of a quart of milk. His day had gone from bad to worse in a span of seconds.

The wet spray burned every orifice and pore on his face. Not wanting to get more in his eyes, Murphy tried to focus on squeezing his eyelids shut, but it was impossible. All plans were out the window the moment that first taste of spray hit your nostrils and throat. He coughed and spit while the pepper spray wreaked havoc on his respiratory system and the baton strikes continued to find their home on various *non-lethal* points of his body.

Eventually, the officer with the baton grew tired of beating Murphy and placed him in handcuffs.

As bad as Murphy had gotten it from the officers, he was apparently in better condition than Spencer. He heard a radio crackle, and an officer called medical personal to the housing area for an inmate who'd been pummeled in a fight and needed immediate medical attention. Spencer was breathing, but unresponsive, they said.

The pepper spray burned Murphy's eyes, preventing him from opening them, so as the officers escorted him from the housing area, he never saw Reese standing in the corner.

Watching.

CHAPTER FOUR

The segregation unit was set up in a *U* shape, three sections, with each area kept independent of the other by a large, steel door which allowed inmates to be housed together, while still keeping enemies or potential problems apart. Each of the three sections had two levels, one ground level, and one up a set of stairs. Murphy had been placed on the lower level at his discipline hearing and had been hammered with the maximum amount allowable under state law—ninety days. Ninety days locked up in a damp, dimly lit cell with no human contact aside from the occasional officer walking through the unit, and the one hour of day the inmates could leave the cell for *recreation*, if you could even call it that. For inmates placed in disciplinary units, recreation consisted of being placed in handcuffs and escorted to cages, which were essentially giant dog kennels outside the unit. The cages were not technically outside—they were in the middle of the area, and there was no overhead roof in that section, which allowed natural sunlight to seep into the rec area, but it was a far cry from actually being outside.

A prison within the prison.

Inmates could spend one hour a day, Monday through

Friday, inside the recreation cage with a few other inmates, so long as they were well behaved. Further infractions within the segregation unit resulted in a loss of recreation privileges and, depending on the infraction, more disciplinary time.

Murphy didn't bother going to the cages. He didn't have any enemy issues with any of the other inmates currently housed in segregation, but that didn't mean he liked any of them, either. He was of the mind to do his time in the box by himself, reading and writing to keep his thoughts from wandering.

Murphy liked to remain optimistic, and the one up-side to being housed in the unit cells were larger cells that only had one bunk. No need to worry about having a nasty pig for a roommate. The extra space gave him more room to do his cell workouts. It sucked, being in the box, but if you could figure out a way to pass the time without losing your mind, it wasn't nearly as bad as Hollywood portrayed it. That being said, some men simply couldn't compartmentalize their brains in a way conducive to passing the time and ended up going what Murphy liked to call *soft in the brain*. There was something a tad bit *off* with men who'd done too much time in the box and couldn't hack it.

Murphy had met a few men like that since getting locked up and didn't want to be one of them, so he did his best to occupy his mind.

A week had passed since the fight, and Murphy was getting a little stir crazy. He'd finished all the books he'd checked out from the library cart quicker than he'd expected and it hadn't come back around, so when it *did* eventually arrive, he was ecstatic. It stopped in front of his cell, and he slipped the books he wanted to return through the feeding tray slot. Once they had been removed by the inmate pushing the cart, he pointed out a few more he wanted to read. The inmate handed them to Murphy through the tray and continued to work his way through the area. With some new books to read, his mental state would improve, he was already feeling better. The ability to get lost in someone else's world made sure he didn't have to remain trapped in his current reality. He flipped through the pages of a book by a man named Aron Beauregard, *Wedding Day Massacre*. It had some sick illustrations in it, so Murphy thought he'd read that one first. As he went to place the book on the shelf, it slipped out of his hand and a loose piece of paper fell from between the pages.

With a grunt, he reached down and picked up both the book and the paper. He placed the book on his shelf and unfolded the paper. It struck him as odd, finding the paper within the pages as he had. Usually, an officer would flip through the books before the cart went around for the sole purpose of making sure no inmates were passing around correspondence through the books. He furrowed his brow, wrinkling his forehead. Murphy was no engineer, but to him, the paper looked like building schematics.

What were building schematics doing inside of a book?

Adding to the peculiarity of the situation—the plans were labeled Glenwood Correctional Institute. But that couldn't be right. Something was off about them. The landmarks surrounding the building on the schematics appeared the same, but there were definitely some rooms on the schematics that didn't exist in the facility, as Murphy knew it. He also noticed there were rooms *not* included in the schematics that he'd seen for himself.

That sparked a memory, something he'd heard someone talking about, but it hadn't crossed his mind at first because the Murphy family hadn't been Glenwood natives, they'd moved to Glenwood a year after their son was born, in search of the perfect place to raise him. What a mistake that had been.

Hadn't the prison been rebuilt a while back? These must be the old plans, Murphy thought.

Initially, Murphy put the plans away. Finding them was certainly unexpected, but they were nothing worth keeping. They were contraband that would see him in further trouble. But his mind kept coming back to them. Something about the schematic called to him, and before he knew it, he spent days wracking his brain over the plans, stopping only for necessary bodily functions. Eating, bathroom breaks, and showers. But even those, he pushed aside until he simply couldn't wait any longer. It had become an unhealthy obsession, one that he couldn't explain. Everything else was put on the back burner, and Murphy spent his time studying the wrinkled sheet of paper, yellowed with time, like an ancient artifact. In some ways, that's exactly what it was. At least as far as things in prison went. And while it may not have been *ancient*, the more Murphy studied it, the more he became convinced his initial assessment had been correct. In his possession, he had the schematics for the old Glenwood Correctional facility, the building that had stood in this very spot prior to its destruction.

Eventually, he had the plans committed to memory. But still, he kept the paper despite knowing the risk of being caught with it. While the plans didn't match up completely with the prison as it stood today, there were more than enough similarities they would likely charge him with possession of escape paraphernalia. Being caught with something like that could mean years in segregation, and likely being classified to a super-max facility once his seg time was served.

Any time Murphy knew he'd be leaving his cell, he folded the plans as small as he could, wrapped them in toilet paper and stuffed the wad between his ass cheeks. The last thing he needed was for an officer to toss his cell searching for contraband while he was at an attorney visit, or next door in the medical unit. It was a great deal of trouble for a piece of paper, but if what he saw on that sheet of paper was correct, the schematics showed something that would be worth a great deal to the inmate population of Glenwood.

A way out.

After pouring countless hours into studying it, and committing it to memory, he came to the realization that there was a basement in the old facility, one that had been built over when the new facility was constructed.

What if that basement were still there? They couldn't have possibly filled it up, could they?

The basement presented an entrepreneurial opportunity for Murphy. Information like what he possessed was unheard of and would fetch quite the prison retail value. No more smoking cigarettes that had been smuggled in through someone's asshole. Filters cut off to make the bundle smaller. He could be the "richest" inmate in the facility if he discovered a way to monetize this escape route. Murphy could only imagine what some inmates would pay to learn about this route. To learn that if someone were to find a way to dig into the basement, they could follow a large drain tunnel that appeared to empty about a mile and a half east of the complex. The more Murphy thought about it, it wasn't a matter of *if* the basement was still there. It had to be. It was a matter of what was the best method of breaking *into* it.

Murphy continued studying the piece of paper. The possibilities were endless.

CHAPTER FIVE

ichelle Murphy stood in front of the kitchen sink, absentmindedly staring out the window with tears carving streaks down her cheeks. Water poured out of the faucet. She hadn't even noticed that she'd dropped the plate. Jagged shards of dish littered the stainless steel, teetering on the edge of the drain. The stress of day-to-day life was becoming too much to bear. The pressure had been steadily building for years, starting before they'd discovered the horrors committed against their son, continuing long after. A never-ending perpetual loop of life beating the shit out of the Murphy family.

Before they'd learned the truth of what happened to their son, Billy, there were warning signs that something wasn't quite right. There usually are, with such atrocities, but warning signs can be easy to miss when you aren't actively looking out for them. And why *would* you be on the lookout for signs that something horrific had happened? Because nobody *ever* thinks it can happen to their family until it does, at which point it's too late and everyone is left scratching their heads, asking themselves, *why us?*

But hindsight is 20/20. Their sweet Billy had suddenly become secretive and much less inclined to talk. He'd always been a motor mouth, so she blamed herself for not noticing right away when that had changed. But sometimes a shift in behavior like that isn't something you pick up on right away. The therapist had even told her as much. Told her it wasn't her fault. It wasn't *anyone's* fault other than the predator responsible for taking his innocence. Still, she couldn't help but feel guilty. It took a while, but eventually she noticed. But even then, Richard had told her it was 'probably just a phase.' Told her she 'worried too much.' For as much as Michelle blamed herself, she blamed her husband more. Motherly instincts told her something was wrong, but she allowed her concerns to be downplayed by her husband until she submitted to him, falling into that old, outdated family dynamic. The misogynistic *father knows best* stereotype.

If only she had only trusted her instincts instead of acquiescing to his misogyny, maybe they could have helped Billy sooner. Things continued without any further changes to the status quo, until suddenly, further behavioral issues arose. When that happened, she really beat the drum that something was wrong. Suddenly her little boy had become a lit fuse, and would lash out at the drop of a dime. He became further withdrawn. Always a B student, his grades suddenly dropped off a cliff and he no longer wanted to participate in the town's youth baseball program. Michelle thought that especially odd, Billy had always loved baseball but seemingly out of nowhere he loathed the sport, had even ripped the posters of his favorite players off his bedroom wall.

It soon came to light Billy's love for the game had soured because his coach was a monster disguised as a human, hiding in plain sight. A man who had seemed like the perfect role model for a young boy, dedicating his spare time to teaching local youth how to play America's favorite pastime.

A man who gained the trust of families before ruining their children's lives.

The monster was eventually apprehended and sentenced to prison, which should have ended the ordeal. But wounds like those inflicted on the Murphy family don't heal properly. The scabs begin to itch until someone picks them and rips the wound open again.

Richard Murphy ripped their scab off, bleeding their family dry.

The criminal justice system decided the monster had learned his lesson, granting him an early release on parole for good behavior. He'd taken a sex offender class and completed it without issue and somehow, they had decided that upon completion, magically, he had been reformed and was no longer a threat to society. Just like that, a few classes and some asshole in a suit and tie gets to decide a child predator's sickness healed, as if there wasn't something irreparably broken inside of a person who got off on children.

Michelle was too emotionally drained to feel anything, but the same couldn't be said for her husband. Richard was furious. He petitioned the parole board, sent letters to the state, spoke on local news channels trying to spark awareness in hopes that the decision would be overturned, but it made no difference. The predator was once again a free man.

So, Richard took matters into his own hands.

He hadn't been thinking about the ramifications of vigilante justice, hadn't considered the consequences of his actions. In his mind, he was simply out to correct a mistake made by the arm of the state.

Michelle couldn't say she disagreed with her husband that the bastard deserved didn't deserve parole, but that was as far as their beliefs ran parallel. She didn't think it was any man's decision to take matters into their own hands. The monster had served his time, and whether he should have served more wasn't something that Michelle had any input on, so she let it go and focused on what was important. All that mattered to her was taking care of Billy.

Richard couldn't cast the past aside, though. He hadn't even bothered hiding his intentions, but Michelle thought her husband was speaking from a place of frustration. She thought it would blow over, like his anger had on so many prior occasions. And if it didn't? She'd talk him off a ledge. It wouldn't be the first time she'd have to calm her husband down, and it probably wouldn't be the last.

Despite her willingness to move on, there was still a part of her that wanted the predator to suffer, but in the end, Michelle was smart enough to know how that one would end. Billy needed his parents to be there for him, not avenge him. Taking action would do nothing but reopen the scars.

What Billy needed was stability from the two people whose job it was to provide such a thing.

What Richard Murphy decided on was revenge.

With the deed done, Billy was fatherless, and Michelle was forced to play the role of Mother, Father, and protector. But now, she wasn't so sure about playing protector. Shortly after her husband was convicted of first-degree murder, Michelle began to experience unease. A sense of impending dread that she couldn't seem to shake. She saw potential catastrophe everywhere. In her mind, simple pranks had nefarious intent. Ding dong ditches were attempts at home invasions. New cars driving through the neighborhood were relatives of the monster out for a little revenge of their own, or another diddler looking for a child to molest. Every man seeking a woman to assault and rape.

Michelle wanted to tell her husband what the stress was doing to her. How being alone, forced to carry the full weight of the consequences of everyone else's actions, along with her duty to Billy, made her feel paranoid, helpless to defend their son. She felt depressed and hopeless. At times, suicidal. But Richard hadn't called her since she'd gone off on him about his delay in telling her about the denial of his parole. At first, she thought he must be upset about the way she'd spoken to him, so she waited a few days to give him some space to clear his mind. But she soon got bored waiting and decided it was time for a face-to-face conversation. Michelle made the two-hour drive to Glenwood Correctional Institute, hoping to pay her husband a visit, only to be turned away at the door.

Inmates in segregation weren't allowed phone calls or visitation rights. The only contact she'd have with her husband for the next few weeks would be good old-fashioned snail mail. *What had gotten into him?* She'd never known Richard to be a violent man, but here he was, in prison for first degree murder and now for what she was told was a brutal assault on another inmate. Clearly, the man she'd married had changed, or had pulled the wool over her eyes, masking his true nature from her.

There were some days—more frequently as of late—where she regretted saying "I do."

Above her, she heard a laugh track from some sitcom Billy was watching. It brought her back to the present. She'd gotten lost in her thoughts, finally allowing herself to drown in the emotions she'd pent up for so long trying to be strong for Billy. With the onslaught of emotion behind her, she could focus on her son once more. He'd been let down too many times and she wouldn't fail him again. Even if it meant putting her own mental and physical well-being aside. Once Billy healed, she could heal.

She had to tell her husband how she was feeling. It would be good to get it out, to write the words down, bleed on the page. Michelle wrote her husband a letter. She withheld some of her feelings, still wanting to speak with him. Some things were better said, not written, allowing her to more easily express her feelings, making sure they weren't lost on the page. Hopefully, he'd call her when he was released from the disciplinary confinement unit. If not, she'd make the drive again.

Michelle's loneliness caused conflicting emotions to battle for dominance. She loathed him for what he'd forced his wife and son to endure, but she was tired of being alone, tired of feeling like everything was up to her. She missed having a partner to deal with life's curveballs.

CHAPTER SIX

The sound of the food tray slot being yanked open startled Murphy awake. He couldn't remember falling asleep. His body was so exhausted he'd simply laid down for a moment and nature took its course. His body ached, stiff from sleeping on a shitty mattress. It screamed for proper nourishment and sleep, but how could he sleep when he had chanced upon such a fascinating discovery? The more he thought about the old, dirty paper, the more it wriggled its way into his brain like a parasite invading a host.

The officer that slammed the food slot open shoved a plastic tray across it. The tray slid across the slot, stopping at the edge of the slot where it hung, dangerously close to flipping over and spilling its contents across the floor. Murphy leapt off the bed, ignoring his body as it screamed at him and rushed across the cell to retrieve the tray before it toppled over. Not that the food was anything special, but he was starving and had no desire to play janitor in his cell so soon after waking. Besides, without a mop and cleaning chemicals to do the job properly, the scent would attract pests. Roaches and mice already ruled the night in the segregation unit.

Murphy saw no need to further entice them. He didn't need any unwanted roommates.

He reached for the tray just as gravity worked its magic, snatching it from the air before it splattered. As he rescued the tray from catastrophe, the officer that had shoved it through the slot tossed a single piece of mail through the same opening. The edge of the envelope struck him in his bare chest, leaving a small dimple where it poked the flesh. Murphy placed the tray on the small writing table that was bolted to the wall and bent over to retrieve the letter. He stopped before picking it up. The handwriting on the envelope was that of his wife. Seeing an unexpected letter from her caused him to freeze. How long had it been since they'd had communication of any kind? Murphy didn't know. Off the top of his head, he couldn't recall how many days he'd been locked up in segregation.

Fuck, I forgot to write to her this entire time. I've been so wrapped up with the schematics. She probably thinks I'm dead. Once she realizes I'm not, she's gonna kill me herself.

Murphy slid the letter out of the envelope. There was no need to tear it open. The mail room officer did that to every single piece of mail prior to delivering it. It was the only way to ensure contraband didn't come in through the mail, and even then, drugs still found a way in all the time. He sniffed the letter. Usually Michelle sprayed it with perfume, but this one had no such accouterments. Unfolding the letter, he noticed the usual long, looping script of her handwriting was replaced with quick scratches of a pen. Some points in the letter were almost nothing more than a scribble. Something was clearly wrong; this letter had been written in haste or under duress. Murphy sat on his bunk and, as he took in the contents of the letter, his heart sank steadily into his chest.

Richard,

I just found out you're in disciplinary confinement. A fight, they tell me. At first, I was pissed because I thought you were blowing me because of our argument, I can't help the way I feel, my only regret is how I said it, but you'll need to excuse me for my lack of tact, I'm hanging on by a thread and you'll never understand just how bad you fucked us. I've tried to hold things together. I've been a faithful wife and caring mother, but I don't know how long I can do this. I'm lonely, and I don't feel safe. Everywhere I go, I see a pedophile waiting to snatch our son or a would-be attacker out for revenge because of what you did. Some family member who believes in an eye for an eye, much the same way you do. I've considered getting a gun, but what would be the point? I don't know how to use one; I don't want to kill anyone. I'm not a monster like you are. Even if I learned how to shoot, there's still a chance that I accidentally kill someone if I'm constantly jumping at shadows, assuming the worst of every stranger I come across. Every day is a struggle to take care of our son, make ends meet, and keep my shit together. Why did you have to leave us? Why? The more I'm here alone, dealing with the consequences of your actions, the angrier I get. I don't know what to do anymore. Billy's childhood was ripped away from him, then his father was ripped away from him and I'm here by myself, trying to pick up the pieces of the mess that everyone made of our lives. Call me. Please. If you care about Billy, find a way to call me. Tell me how we fix this. I don't know that we can.

Michelle

Murphy stared at the letter. So many thoughts swirled through his mind at once.

Hurt. Anger. Sadness.

He knew he fucked up bad when he killed the diddler, and as much as he'd plotted and planned to take that piece of shit's life, as much as he couldn't see a past where he *didn't* put a bullet in that piece of shit, he had never once considered the repercussions it would have on his family. Maybe he wasn't the illustrious father he had always thought he was. If he was even *half* that good, at some point he would have considered the impact his actions could have on his family. But he didn't. Instead, he had been consumed with a revenge family until he'd acted.

Murphy laid down on his bunk and tried to go back to sleep, tried to shut his brain off, but he couldn't. Not now, not after reading the heartbreaking letter from Michelle. Clearly, she was going through some shit, and it was his fault. He couldn't blame that piece of shit child molester for all of his family's troubles. The man had made his mark, that's for sure, but Murphy couldn't put all the blame on him. This one was all on him. *God have mercy on my soul.*

He lay on the bunk for hours, unable to think of a plan. What could he say? What could he do to make his wife feel better? She was right. For him, every day was groundhog day, but for his wife and kid, time had continued its breakneck pace. Bills didn't stop for them simply because Murphy was locked up. Doctor appointments, parent-teacher conferences, preventative maintenance on their vehicles—all routine things in daily life that continued to be necessary, and while he was here feeling sorry for himself, his wife was at home getting shit done. His own mind wouldn't give him a break, reminding him what a fucking idiot he was. Yes, a monster had upended the lives of the Murphy clan, but it was Richard Murphy himself who'd replaced their boogeyman by becoming a murdering monster himself, ensuring they would never recover from the damage done.

That was something he would have to live with for the rest of his life.

Eventually, exhaustion claimed victory over the restlessness of his mind and Murphy passed out.

When Murphy woke, he had no clue the time, or how long he'd been asleep for. The overhead lights in the hallway were off, as were the lights in his cell. The officer in the segregation control unit could turn the lights in each individual cell on and off, as well as the lights in the hallway with just a few button presses. Midnight was usually lights out for the unit, the only source of illumination from that point on were the "night lights" within each cell—nothing more than a dimmer version of the main light in the cell.

But not tonight. Even those were off, and Murphy could hardly see his own hand when held up in front of his face. It was possible the facility had lost power, but even then, there was a backup generator that ran on diesel and kicked in automatically in the event of an outage.

Something was wrong. Different. In a place like this, different was never good.

Heavy footfalls echoed down the hallway, reverberating off the walls, the sound amplified in the darkness. Drops of water dripped from the open-air shower next to his cell, pinging off the hard cement floor. The noise was torturous when trying to sleep, but here, in the dark, it set the small hairs on his neck on end. Murphy listened closely, trying to gauge where the footfalls were headed. It had to be late, or early, depending on how you looked at it. Even with all the lights off, if daylight hours there would be *some* ambient light coming through from the small crack at the top of the cell wall that constituted a window.

The footsteps grew louder before eventually stopping in front of Murphy's cell. He heard a voice whisper, "You've got 10 minutes," followed by another hushed voice, "Not gonna take that long."

The first voice, "Don't forget, you owe me."

"I don't owe you shit. Don't forget who runs this mother-fucker. That badge doesn't mean shit around here. It would be a shame if little Jimmy didn't make it home from school, don't you think?"

"You fucking piece of shit. I did what you asked…"

"Relax fuck face, get me in that cell and nobody is gonna touch him."

Murphy had no clue what was going on, but he knew enough about Glenwood to know the number one way inmates got correction officers to do fucked up shit was to threaten their families. It sounded an awful lot to him, like someone was about to enter his cell and there was no way in hell anything good could come from that.

He hopped off his bunk, slipped on his shoes, and put his back against the wall, all within a few seconds. The cell door slid open as he raised his fists in the air, ready for anything. The cell door slammed shut as quickly as it had opened, the loud metal clang deafening in the otherwise silent area. Someone was here, but who? It was still too dark to see across the cell, even after his eyes had acclimated to the absence of light.

The sound of footsteps came once again as the intruder stalked forward. "Hey there, Richie. You mind if I call you Richie? You think you're a real bad mother fucker don't ya? You must have lost your goddamned mind if you think I'm gonna let you put one of my boys in the hospital the way you did and you just get to stay in segregation like a bitch and not get what's coming to you. You like being a bitch, Richie? Because I'm about to make you mine. From now on, your new name is Richelle, and you're my bitch, so bend over for daddy, Richelle."

Reese's words set Murphy over the edge. He charged at Reese, ready to pummel the life out of the racist, bigot piece of shit.

It was the last thing he should have done, all things considered, but Reese must have been smart enough to know what Murphy lacked in stature compared to him, he made up for in brains and cunning. Poking the bear, angering Murphy enough to throw caution to the wind, effectively removed Murphy's biggest advantage.

Murphy closed the gap with a few quick steps and launched himself through the air, throwing a superman punch at Reese. The bigger man easily sidestepped the blow and Murphy sailed past him, landing on the ground with a thud. He tucked his knees at the last second, using his momentum to roll forward, narrowly avoiding Reese's counter-attack—a well-aimed kick that would have otherwise connected with the back of Murphy's head.

Murphy stood up, reorienting himself, squaring up with Reese. Staying on the offensive, he made the first move again. But this time, he did so in a calculated manner, not letting his temper overwhelm him. Any mistake could cost him his life. A left-handed jab, a quick flick of a punch, connected with Reese's nose. Blood ran from Reese's nostril. The punch wasn't meant to do significant damage, but to distract Reese from defending against the straight right hand that followed the quick punch. And it would have worked, but Reese was an experienced fighter, he'd been to this rodeo far too many times to *not* expect punches in bunches, so after getting tagged with the first shot he immediately moved his head off-center, slipping the follow up and countering with a left hook to Murphy's ribs.

The counterpunch landed on the money.

The meaty slap of flesh on flesh echoed through the small cell and the impact of the blow forced the oxygen to rush out of Murphy's lungs with an *oof* sound. It felt like someone had hit him with a baseball bat. Murphy did his best to mask the pain, aside from having the wind knocked out of him. He didn't want Reese to know when he caught him good; the man was a predator and if he knew Murphy was a wounded animal, he'd surely go in for the kill.

Following Reese's clubbing blow to his ribs, Murphy

dropped his right elbow slightly in order to better defend against another body shot, which is exactly what Reese followed up with. The blow, thrown to the same area, landed hard against Murphy's elbow, crushing the ulnar nerve against the humerus bone. A sharp, tingling pain shot through his arm. It was horrible luck that the punch landed in that exact spot, but he didn't have time to think about it. Instinctively, he shook his arm out, trying to shake off a pain that would burn bright for moments, but quickly dissipate.

Reese pounced on Murphy's momentary lapse of defense, throwing two more left hooks to the body that landed flush, right in the spot Murphy's arm had been moments before. He followed them up with an overhand right haymaker. It connected flush on Murphy's chin in a downward arc, driving him to the ground.

Reese jumped on Murphy, throwing punch after punch. Many of them didn't land clean because Murphy covered up like a turtle in his shell. But Reese was a large man and each blow from his swarming attack chipped away at Murphy's defense and stamina until he was too exhausted to even shell up any longer.

The attack ceased, but if Reese was winded, he gave no indication. His breathing was normal, no wheezing, as if he hadn't just rained hellfire down on his opponent. Murphy lay on the ground bleeding, blood bubbling from his mouth as the heavy, labored breaths passed through his lips. He tried to crawl away, but moving even a few inches was too much for his battered frame.

Reese grabbed Murphy by his long, dark brown hair, squeezing tight. He dragged Murphy to the corner of the cell and dropped him in front of the toilet. His fingers hovered momentarily at the waistband of his orange jumpsuit. "I told you I was going to make you my bitch, Richelle," Reese said as he dropped his pants and boxers to his ankles in one smooth motion. His long, thick cock stood at attention, and he licked his hand before sliding it up and down, helmet to shaft, lubricating his weapon with saliva and pre-cum.

With one hand stroking his member, Reese grabbed Murphy by the hair once more and hefted him over the toilet. Reese's upper chest lay across the bowl, the hard surface crushing Murphy's sternum while supporting his weight.

Murphy struggled to get free, but he'd been beaten too badly to muster any real resistance. He wouldn't beg for Reese's mercy. The man had none. He was a monster, and Murphy wouldn't give him the satisfaction of begging. Sick fucks like him fed on the power, it made them feel important. He'd take what Reese had as quietly as possible and, if luck was on his side, live to fight another day.

Reese pressed hard on the back of Murphy's head, keeping him in place as he thrust, ramming his huge cock—slick with saliva and pre-cum—into Murphy's virgin asshole. A hot poker of pain pierced his anus as his rectum tore. Reese pounded away and Murphy's entire body went rigid from the searing pain brought on from the beating his anus was taking. The pain and exhaustion he had felt moments before couldn't hold a candle to the pain, fear, and shame overwhelming him as he was violated.

Too battered to resist, Murphy tried escaping from the moment mentally, tried to force an out-of-body experience, but he couldn't bring his mind to his happy place—the water park with his son. It was his favorite memory and when times got tough, he reminisced, retreating into the memory. Not now though, Reese's animalistic grunts as he raped Murphy kept him anchored in the moment, rendering him unable to escape.

He no longer wanted to live to fight another day. He wished Reese would kill him, waited for death's cold embrace.

"You like that, you little bitch?" Reese grunted.

Behind them, the cell door slid open with a grinding metal

sound that momentarily halted Reese's fevered thrusts. "Time's up, Reese," a hushed voice said.

"Gimme a second."

Reese started pumping away again, quicker this time, pounding Murphy's asshole until he abruptly stopped, gripping Murphy tightly while his ejaculate spurted out.

"I said, let's fucking go," the officer said as he took his baton in a double fisted grip, bringing it over Reese's head and lowering it to his throat. The officer yanked Reese backward, strangling him as he dragged the skinhead across the ground, pants at his ankles, heels sliding across the floor.

Reese tried to talk but the only sound that escaped was garbled nonsense, the baton crushing his trachea as he was extracted from the cell by the same man that had permitted him access earlier.

The cell door slammed shut once more, locking Murphy away in the dark with nothing but shame to keep him company. With nobody around to keep a facade for, Murphy broke. He wept on the floor until he passed out; the darkness dragging him into a restless sleep.

The days turned into weeks, and Murphy hardly knew of their passing. He stopped taking showers, refused any recreation time. Following the assault, Murphy didn't eat for the first few days, and he even held his bowel movements for fear that taking a shit would open up the wound, physically and mentally. He tried so hard to forget the pain, he couldn't risk experiencing it again. Eventually, he could hold it no longer. Nature took its course and Murphy was relieved to discover the bowel movement was pain free. Still, he only ate one meal a day. The sexual assault took something from him mentally and it took everything he had to not end it right then and there. Staff noticed the odd change in his behavior and placed him on suicide watch, but after a few days passed with no attempts at self-harm, they interviewed Murphy, clearing him of suicide watch. He never mentioned the assault. Rats in Glenwood Correctional Institute had a short life expectancy and although he had wished for death the night of the assault, he didn't want to bring further trouble to himself.

Footsteps echoed down the hall and Murphy went rigid. Blood coursed through his veins, and he clenched his fists. He was ready to fight, but when the footsteps stopped at his cell, it turned out to be an officer passing out dinner trays. A clear, plastic tray slid through the opening in the middle of his door and the officer spoke. "Time's up buddy. You're going back to population tomorrow. Hope you had a good time," he said, chuckling to himself and continuing down the line of cells. Murphy's blood boiled. *Was that the piece of shit who let Reese in?* It didn't matter. He couldn't do anything about it, anyway. Better to not know the truth because he might do something he'd regret later on.

He stood up, making his way to the cell door and grabbed the tray from the slot, lifting the lid as he brought it to the small desk welded to the wall. Spicy chicken tenders on the menu tonight. The smell stung his nostrils, and his stomach growled. He'd eat this meal, although he'd regret it. Murphy could never turn down spicy foods, despite the acid reflux he was guaranteed to experience later, and the way it would burn coming out the other end after his body digested it. Thank God for the cartons of milk they pass out with dinner. He'd need it to tame the acidic burn that would be sure wreak havoc on his esophagus. Murphy devoured the entire tray in minutes and placed it back in the slot where it would sit until the inmate working the area collected the trays.

Murphy lay back down on the bunk and closed his eyes,

willing sleep to come. Better to sleep the days away than live like an animal locked in a cage.

The squeaking wheels of the library cart echoed through the dark corridor, waking Murphy from his sleep. He sat upright, unaware of how much time had passed. It had to be late; the nightlights were on. *Why would the library cart be making rounds now?* It made little sense. The cart always made its rounds during the morning shift. They'd already eaten dinner, and all inmates returned to their cells by 8:30 each night.

Whether or not it made sense didn't change the fact. It *was* the library cart, and that for some reason it was stopped right in front of his cell.

The inmate pushing the cart stepped in front of the cart, placing his body right against the door. A shit-eating grin smeared across his face. Murphy didn't recognize the inmate. Not only could he not place a name to the face, but he was positive he'd never seen the man prior to this moment. The inmate was tall, slightly chubby, and had pale skin spotted with freckles. The longer Murphy observed him, the more the man's complexion didn't seem just pale, but looked flat out unhealthy, like he hadn't seen the sun in decades. A generous mop of curly orange hair adorned his head. It made Murphy immediately think of the comedian, Carrot Top. The name tag stitched across Carrot Top's chest read *O'Rourke.*

Now, Murphy was positive he didn't know the man. Realistically it was impossible for Murphy to know every inmate housed in the facility, but he knew most of them and O'Rourke looked so sickly he was sure he'd have remembered meeting the man. And that name, so stereotypically

Irish, he'd have remembered hearing it around. He supposed O'Rourke could be a new commit, but if that *were* the case, how had he gotten a cushy job like inmate librarian so soon? A job like that was reserved for men doing big time who'd proven over the course of their sentence that they could be trusted as much as staff could trust an inmate, at least. With a position like librarian, it would be far too easy to pass contraband within books and hide them away within the shelves of the library—a place the officers rarely went, never mind searched.

"Gonna need that reading material back now," said O'Rourke.

"I'm not finished with the book, though."

O'Rourke smiled again. "I didn't say anything about a book. I said that reading material."

Murphy's blood ran cold. *He couldn't be talking about the plans, could he?*

Feigning ignorance, Murphy said, "All I've got is this one book. I've had it most of the time I've been in here. I've been reading slowly, as of late."

"Don't play with me, Murphy. I know everything that goes on here. I'm the librarian of this place. I deal with nothing but knowledge. As I said, it's time to return your reading material," O'Rourke said, waving a familiar slip of paper in front of Murphy's cell door.

"What the fuck? How did you..." Murphy picked the book up and flipped through the pages. The map was gone, but how? He flipped the book on its side, shaking it so the pages flapped, expecting the map to fall out.

No such luck. It had vanished.

Murphy crossed the cell, pressing against the door. "How did you get that?" he hissed.

"Like I said, kid, you're done with it. Your time is up. It goes back in the cart."

"Where did it come from?"

"It came from here. Things have a funny way of disappearing and turning up around here. This is a very, very old place. The original building stood for hundreds of years before they torched it in the riot. Imagine, if you will, the amount of pain, suffering, despair, and death that happens in a place such as this over the span of the facility's lifetime. By default, prisons are terrible places, and when you put enough bad in one spot, it becomes a magnet for evil. If that map found you, there's a reason for it, and you've got to think that maybe whatever set you on the path to finding it didn't do it for altruistic reasons. It can take you where you need to go, yes, but why would it *want* you to get there? What's the toll on a route paved in blood?" O'Rourke turned around and began pushing the cart away.

Murphy pounded his fist against the cell door. O'Rourke was talking in riddles. What the fuck was this guy's deal?

"Listen, man, I don't need a damn map out of this place. I'm not going anywhere until they let me out. So why the cryptic shit? I don't *need* to go anywhere. What the fuck does that even mean?"

O'Rourke spun around and grabbed the bars, pressing his face into them. He was now eye to eye with Murphy.

Murphy jumped back, his heart jack hammered in his chest, and he cried out. O'Rourke's features had undertaken a macabre transformation. Half of his skull was caved in, brain exposed. Maggots wriggled along the chasm in his skull, feasting on dead, rotting brain matter. A few of them fell from their perch, plopping onto the food tray flap of his cell. The hideous creature that had been O'Rourke was missing its left eye. Where the eye should have been was an empty socket filled with more insects—millipedes, beetles, cockroaches. His skin still screamed of pallor mortis, but was now covered with deep purple bruises. One side of his mouth was sliced open from the corner of the lips to the jaw hinge, exposing the few decaying teeth left in the corpse's mouth. Strands of connective tissue seemed to be the only thing holding the jaw in place.

Through its mangled face, O'Rourke spoke in a harsh, whispered rattle, "It means exactly what it fucking sounds like, Murphy. When they rebuilt this place over the ruins of the old facility, the *evil* didn't just go away. The warden was a manifestation of that evil, of darkness. When the warden's physical vessel was destroyed in the riots, the few remaining inmates and officers that knew what was really going on thought they had stopped the darkness. But they stopped nothing. Evil doesn't die. It can't die. It can dissipate, it can move on, you can even take away its strength, but you can't kill it and its strength always comes back, eventually. What they did all those years ago was cap a pipe. Eventually the pressure will build up and the pipe will burst, Glenwood will be a much worse place once that happens. Evil is a funny thing. It latches on to people, on to things. Have you ever heard the stories of the Maniac of D Block, correctional officer Lee Harris? He was a real son of a bitch. A no good piece of shit correction officer. He'd earned that distinction even before the darkness arrived here in the form of the warden. Even the nickname, *The Maniac,* was a moniker he'd earned before evil had truly arrived. The Maniac had a penchant for beating the shit out of inmates. He'd even killed a few and gotten away with it. And when the darkness here grew, it fed on him, and he fed on it until they both grew stronger. What people don't know about the riot is The Maniac was responsible for more deaths, inmate and officer alike, than any other person who'd had the misfortune of being at Glenwood Correctional Institute when shit popped off. He'd used the riot as his opportunity to kill, unchecked. When the building went up in flames and crumbled around him, Lee was presumed dead."

O'Rourke stopped talking, turned around and pushed the

cart down the hall, leaving Murphy to digest what O'Rourke had told him.

Murphy called out, "What do you mean, presumed dead? They never recovered a body?" He thought about what O'Rourke said. *Evil doesn't die.*

The walking corpse, O'Rourke, was gone. Vanished without answering Murphy's question.

His head spun. He felt nauseous. Clearly, he'd spent too much time locked in this cell and was losing his mind. That had to be it. What other explanation could there be? He'd been locked up, stuck in his own head, and now he'd become a statistic. Another number for the studies on inmate mental health. One more person to add to the list of names lawmakers would use as ammunition in their pushes to get rid of disciplinary confinement all together. Murphy didn't think that was going to happen. He'd been in prison long enough to know that there were just some men who couldn't be around other people. They were a danger to themselves, and a danger to others. But sitting here in the dark, talking to dead men? Maybe they had a point. Maybe segregation really did make men go crazy. Either that, or he was having one hell of a nightmare.

He lay back on his bunk, scared shitless. There would be no sleep the rest of the night.

CHAPTER SEVEN

The sun rose high in the sky the next day and Murphy was awake to watch the sliver of light through his tiny window, eyes burning with fatigue. After his encounter in the middle of the night, he'd been unable to sleep, try as he might. Every time his eyelids grew so heavy, he couldn't keep them open, visions of O'Rourke flashed before his eyes. His mind conjured images of a correction officer gone mad with power, brutally murdered in a riot, yet somehow the body gone missing. The viciousness of the assault he pictured was likely a consequence of the man's own malicious conduct. Something about that story bugged Murphy. He couldn't be sure what he'd seen. He'd spent too much time locked away in segregation to be confident it wasn't a hallucination. But the idea of evil lurking within Glenwood sent shivers up his spine that were difficult to ignore.

None of it added up. The appearance of O'Rourke, for one, meant Murphy was probably certifiable. And this Lee Harris guy, The Maniac, how was it possible they never discovered his body? Even if the faculty burned to the ground, shouldn't there have been *some* sort of remains? Bones? Clothing? Hell, dental fillings?

Murphy should have been excited, knowing he was about to be released to general population. Instead, he was depressed, exhausted, and terrified. He couldn't close his eyes or his mind, but who could blame him? When you were surrounded by fences, razor wire, and massive steel doors, even the most beautiful day was dreary. You woke up each morning and, if you were smart, attempted to make the most of a shitty situation. But you could only polish a turd so much. You were still locked up. And if that weren't bad enough, Murphy had been isolated for weeks with almost no human contact.

He was a caged animal in the land of the free.

It was something Murphy thought about often.

In a book somewhere in the prison's library, Murphy had read some crazy statistics that had opened his eyes to the country's criminal justice system. America, the country with the most total number of inmates, along with the highest incarceration rate in the world. Roughly twenty-five percent of all incarcerated inmates worldwide were housed in the United States. *Experts* could argue until they were blue in the face about the *how's* and the *why's*, but in the end, it didn't matter.

In life, rarely do things *really* matter. Stats were stats. For as many ACLU types as there were fighting for better conditions and policies in America's criminal justice system, the hard truth was that most people simply didn't give a shit how people locked up lived. *It's prison. Nobody forced you to commit a crime* was the prevailing attitude. But as bad as Glenwood Correctional Institute was, it was common knowledge it had been even worse in the months and years before the riot that ended in the destruction of the entire facility. And Murphy knew as bad things were at Glenwood, there were prisons across the country far worse.

Objectively speaking, Murphy could understand why the vast majority of American citizens didn't give a shit what went down in prisons, how inmates were treated. Why would anyone care about the living conditions of murderers and rapists? If he were honest, some amenities they received would probably shock the average person. Tablets with email and FaceTime access, video game consoles, cable television. Hell, that they were wards of the state meant that many inmates received lifesaving medications and procedures that they simply wouldn't have received had they not been incarcerated. Medications, equipment, and procedures that plenty of law-abiding citizens simply didn't have access to, either. Murphy understood why that would upset people. But was that a prison problem? Or maybe Americans had simply put up with being raped by the medical industry with no help from the government for far too long and accepted that as the standard.

Whether the inmates deserved that level of care, Murphy couldn't say for sure. Sometimes he felt they should have access, and other times where he felt most of the guys in Glenwood deserved every shitty thing that came their way. It was a tough call to make after meeting some of the men here. Men who made the crimes Reese committed seem like nothing more than detention worthy stunts. Men who had committed crimes so despicable, calling them atrocities was an understatement. The type of shit that would make a person lose hope in humanity. Sick things that Murphy thought would cause even the most avid true crime fan to pause.

As far as Murphy was concerned, *those* guys deserved a bullet, not a PlayStation, three warm meals, and access to life saving healthcare.

With his mind preoccupied with O'Rourke, The Maniac, and the United States criminal justice system, Murphy forgot to eat his breakfast. It sat on the edge of the tray slot, untouched, until it was taken away. A few hours after the tray was removed and the sun was at its peak in the sky, they finally released Murphy back to the general population. They'd even sent him back to the same housing unit he'd been in prior to the fight that had landed him in segregation.

Normally Murphy would have considered that a good thing, but Reese lived in the same unit. Now more than ever, each day he was trapped in Glenwood was another day Reese or one of his goons might make an attempt on his life. He'd need to be extra vigilant and do his best to not provoke the skinheads. Living in the same unit would not make that a straightforward task. He tried to look on the bright side. At least being housed in the same unit as Reese would make it easier to monitor the man. Maybe keeping his enemy close would allow him to be better prepared for the inevitable.

Murphy walked up the pathway in the yard all the way back to the housing unit with all his belongings packed into the cart he was pushing. The trek was more difficult than Murphy would have thought, the wheel on the cart broken and spinning sideways.

When he arrived, he was instantly disappointed. The officer had given him his new cell assignment, and it disheartened him to learn that Lewis had a new cellmate. He wasn't surprised. In fact, he'd expected it. With the new commits to Glenwood every day, the population was rapidly expanding, and it was almost for a single occupant to remain in the cell with no roommate for more than a few days. That luxury was reserved for inmates with mental or physical health issues that made having a roommate either improbable, or impossible. Even Reese—a man with half the staff in his back pocket—was forced to double bunk with someone.

Still, a part of him had hoped that Lewis would have somehow convinced the block officer to hold a bunk for him until they released him back to general population.

Entering his new cell, Murphy quickly realized he'd

pulled the short straw. The first thing he noticed was the putrid funk permeating the air. The cell stunk like absolute shit, the funk so overpowering it made him wonder if his new cell mate took showers. Hopefully, the man wasn't one of the crazies that refused to bathe. There were a few guys like that around Glenwood. Men so disgusting, and so averse to personal hygiene that staff were forced to physically place them in a shower for their own health, and for the health of the inmates forced to house with them. The cell was practically barren aside from his cellmates' few belongings—food scraps and dirty laundry. The nasty fucker had even left a fefe—a homemade flesh-light—lying on the floor in the middle of the cell. As for the slob the mess belonged to, he wasn't in the cell. Murphy gave the housing unit a cursory look, scanning for a man who looked trashy enough to live in the filth Murphy was standing in. He didn't see anyone that fit the bill.

A large, red cockroach skittered across Murphy's beat up Timberland work boot. He kicked the roach out of the cell, careful to scoot his foot so he didn't crush the nasty fucker. He shivered. Nothing grossed him out more than the vermin and pests that infested the prison. It was impossible to avoid them no matter what lengths you went to to keep your cell tidy, but a roommate like the nasty bastard he was stuck living with attracted them like flies to shit.

Murphy unpacked his belongings and, just as he finished making his bunk, a haggard, dirty man entered the cell. He stood there watching, unnoticed, as Murphy did his best to organize his belongings. After a few moments of Murphy not noticing the man behind him, the slob coughed, trying to get Murphy's attention. Murphy turned around and locked eyes with the nasty little fucker. Red splotches and dry, flaky pieces of dead skin littered the man's face. He smiled a mostly toothless grin. Murphy could practically see stink lines straight from an illustration wafting out of the man's sewer hole of a mouth. The walking Irish Spring advertisement held out a dirty, grimy hand—a rather disgusting greeting. There was no way in hell Murphy was touching that man's hand. Scabies weren't on his list of things to experience in prison.

Far from a match made in heaven, this living situation simply would not work. The man was every disease wrapped up in a human shell and something needed to change ASAP, and he was pretty sure it wouldn't be the man's personal hygiene. There were only a few ways this scenario could play out going forward. Best-case scenario, he'd find a new cell-mate, hopefully Lewis. If that wasn't an option, he'd strongly suggest to his soup sandwich of a roommate that it would be in his best interest to practice good hygiene. Brushing his teeth, wiping his ass. The basics. If the implied threat of serious bodily injury wasn't enough to convince the slob to shower more often than Murphy would simply beat the shit out of him, do another stint in the box, and when he was released to general population again, he'd be assigned to a new, hopefully more desirable cell.

Murphy looked around the cell block once more. He hadn't seen Lewis since he reported back to the unit and was excited to check in with his friend to see how things were going. Truth be told, he was a bit bummed out that Lewis hadn't stopped by the check in with him. Maybe he was busy at a class or something. After looking around for a bit, Murphy eventually spotted Lewis in the back corner of the housing unit. He was standing next to the phone sipping a plastic cup filled with shitty mix and stir coffee.

Murphy approached Lewis, a grin splitting his face from ear to ear, arms spread in the universal gesture of a hug. Lewis looked him dead in the eyes and said nothing. He didn't return the smile, didn't reciprocate the gesture. Murphy's shoulders slumped; his mood soured at Lewis' lack of excitement.

Lewis nodded his head but broke Murphy's gaze. "What's

up?" he said, after it was clear the reunion was going to be an awkward one.

"What's up? That's all you've got to say? I've been locked in a cage for all this time, and you can't even pretend like you're happy to see me. What's up with *you*?"

"Nothing's up with me, man. I'm good, I just don't want to be bothered is all."

Murphy wasn't buying it. Lewis was acting weird. They'd been close since the first week Murphy arrived at Glenwood. It wasn't like his friend to brush him off the way he had. Wasn't like the man to be *bothered* by his closest friend's presence.

"I was hoping you'd have gotten one of the officers to get me back in the cell with you. I don't have a problem with a top bunk, you know that," Murphy said. "Now, I'm stuck with that gross motherfucker, and not for nothing, but you're acting like you don't even know me. What's the fuckin' deal, man?"

Lewis scratched his head before answering, seemed to think a bit too long about how he wanted to respond. "Yeah, about that. I was thinking maybe I shouldn't fuck with you anymore. Reese is right, you should just keep away from me. Those skinheads, racist fucks don't like me, and I know they're giving you shit about it."

Murphy's face turned red; his ears warmed with shame. Did Lewis know about what happened in segregation? Did Reese tell everyone? Word traveled quick behind bars, but had it spread that quickly?

Lewis continued speaking, made no indication whether or not he knew about the assault. "Reese isn't happy about what you did to his boy," Lewis said. "You know people talk. I heard what happened when you were in the box. You look healed up. I don't want to cause more problems for you, man, that's all. I don't want to give Reese another reason to target you after what you did to his boy."

So, there it was. Lewis knew about the beating. Did he know about the rape, too?

"I get what you're saying, and I appreciate it, but I'm not gonna let those dickheads control my life. Reese and his dogs can get their faces fucked." Murphy said with a stone-faced expression.

"If you say so, man, but don't get mad at me when they come looking for you. Those white boys don't like any of their own to talk to the rest of us."

"I'm not one of them. That's my word."

"I know. You're good people, Murphy. That's why I wanted to keep some space. I know where this goes from here."

"Me too. It is what it is. I'll deal with it when the time comes. So, what do you say? Are we good?"

This time Lewis opened his arms, the only response necessary. They embraced.

"So, what was it like doing that much time? How the fuck did you *not* go crazy in there?" Lewis asked.

Murphy laughed. "Who said I didn't? You ain't gonna believe this shit man, I almost don't believe it myself. Maybe I snapped a bit. Check this shit out," Murphy said.

He motioned for Lewis to follow, and as the two men paced back and forth through the block, Murphy recounted the strange tale. How he'd found building plans tucked away in a book, and how an inmate named O'Rourke that he'd never met before just showed up one day with the library cart and somehow the plans were gone from his cell and reappeared in the man's possession. He even told Lewis the story O'Rourke had told him about the old prison, The Maniac of D Block, Lee Harris, and how O'Rourke had suddenly turned into a festering corpse.

When the story was over, Lewis seemed to have taken the whole thing in stride.

"As bat shit crazy as it sounds, I believe you. I've seen

enough creepy shit go down around this motherfucker to *know* this place is haunted. And why wouldn't it be? How many people have died here over the years? Murders, suicides, natural causes. Nah, you couldn't convince me it's *not* haunted. Truth be told, I've met both O'Rourke and Harris. Not recently, of course, that was decades ago. I was maybe eighteen at the time. But you described O'Rourke how I remember him, before the whole being dead thing, and anyone who'd ever met Harris would remember The Maniac of D Block until the day they died. Hell, I met him before he started doing the *real* fucked up shit he eventually got a rep for, and even back then he was a real son of a bitch. So yeah, it's nuts, but I believe you. And if "evil" was gonna latch on to something, or someone around Glenwood, The Maniac is about as perfect a candidate as you're ever gonna find."

"That's it? Just like that? You don't want proof; you don't want an explanation? You just believe me?"

"Yeah. I don't need any proof. The fact you know about O'Rourke and Harris is pretty fucking telling. Like I said, way too many people have died here, and way too much bad shit happened in this facility, and on the grounds for it to be anything *but* haunted."

"Right, but you're not even a little put off about some psychotic correctional officer somehow fusing with some sort of evil that had been feeding on everything bad that happened here in the old building? It sounds like some shit out of a Bentley Little novel."

"Man, pull your head out of your ass. Of course, I'm put off by that shit. I'm scared to death of some shit like that. But you know what? If that motherfucker has been stuck in the basement this whole time, or wherever the fuck he's at, that means he's not near me, and that's enough to let me fall asleep at night. I'm gonna sit right here in this block, eat my three meals, jerk off to the penthouse forums books I bought, and count the days until I get up out of this bitch again. And when I'm out? I ain't ever coming back, that's for damn sure."

Murphy laughed. "How many times have you said that before?"

Lewis punched Murphy on the shoulder. "Fuck off, man, I mean it this time. Fifty is too old to be fucking around with all these young kids in here. And last time I said it, I didn't have your crazy ass telling me these fucked up stories."

"Shit man, you've got that old man strength, huh?" Murphy rubbed his shoulder. "So, you're really gonna make me live with that smelly ass bum, huh?"

"I'll consider asking the officer if he can move us. Maybe I'll wait until tomorrow, though. I wanna make you really appreciate how clean I keep my area."

"You're a real piece of work, you know that, right?"

The intercom sounded, interrupting their conversation. *All inmates return to your cells. It is count time. All inmates return to your cells and stand for the count.*

"Shit, I didn't realize the time flew by that quick. I'll see you in a few hours," Murphy said.

"Alright. Don't go beating anyone up now. Especially not that fucking gremlin you're living with. It isn't his fault his ass stinks."

"Fuck you, man. If it's not his fault he doesn't wipe his ass, who's fault is it?"

Lewis laughed as he walked into his cell, closing the door behind him. Murphy returned to his own cell, mentally steeling himself for the stench of the old bastard they forced him to room with. Hopefully, he'd be moved in with Lewis by the end of the night. He knew his friend would come through.

CHAPTER EIGHT

R ichard,
I've tried my best to keep everything together while you've been locked up, despite the fact that I have barely been able to hold myself together. I know that what you did, you did out of love for our son. But what you did was wrong and has caused further irreversible damage to our family. Not only was his innocence taken by a monster, but his father was taken from him by that same monster. He's constantly bullied at school. The kids all call him all sorts of nasty names. They tease him about the horrific trauma he was forced to go through. We all know children can be cruel, but that is beyond fucked. Maybe that's why he tried to kill himself last week. Imagine going to school every day when all the other students know what happened to you. I can see why he might have felt like it was his only option. But you didn't know that had happened, did you? Because once again I haven't gotten phone calls or letters from you. Are you in disciplinary confinement again? And if not, why are you avoiding me? Do you have a side chick? I'm starting to think you might be looking for another young, gullible girl dumb enough to believe what you tell her. When I came to visit you that day, they turned me away because you were in segregation. The officer that gave me the bad news also told me you

guys have been known to do that when you're locked up. Play the field with young women with low self-esteem. Is that it? You have your wife at home, holding it down, and a little side bitch that talks dirty to you? Sends you nasty letters and naughty pictures? That's cheating, too, you asshole. It's called emotional cheating. You don't have to stick your little pecker in someone to cheat. You men and your games, you try to play us like chessboards, and now the more I think about it, the more I believe you've got another woman lined up to give you some ass on the side when you get out, because nothing else about your behavior makes sense to me.

So, what's new with your wife and son? Well, for starters I can't even afford the rent anymore now that the savings is dried up. Mr. Vega told me he wouldn't start the eviction process, and I could pay the back rent, along with next month's rent, if I sucked his cock. I told him he can suck MY cock and go ahead and start the process. There's no need for that though, because I won't be here by the time it goes to court, and neither will your son. We're leaving. We're going to find a place somewhere far away and get a fresh start. I don't feel this is a safe place to raise my son anymore, and frankly, I want to start a life for myself and my son that doesn't include you, because I don't think you're safe to be around him, either. Consider us the family you left behind. Don't write. Don't call. We don't want to hear from you.

Michelle.

Murphy screamed. He threw the letter to the floor, picked it up, and read it again. And again. And again.

He couldn't believe the words scrawled across the page. Tears streaming down his cheeks, he crumpled it into a ball and threw it in the corner of the cell. It was a sick joke; it had to be. Someone else had written the letter, a fucked-up prank. Reese. Reese was fucking with him.

He picked the crumpled letter up, unfolded it, and read it once more. Who was he fooling? Reese hadn't pranked him. The handwriting was clearly that of his wife. The words were still there; he hadn't imagined them. Daggers of ink drawing blood as if made from the sharpest metal. His wife had really taken his son and left. When did they leave? He picked up the envelope and checked the date on the post office stamp. It had been postmarked a week ago. They could be anywhere by now. Michelle never mentioned a destination. And why would she? She had made it clear in the letter that they were through, and he wasn't welcome in their lives anymore. But she couldn't do that, could she?

There had to be laws against it. Even if he were incarcerated, there had to be some kind of laws protecting his parental rights. Was this a kidnapping? Maybe, but how was he supposed to get ahold of an attorney on such short notice? With his trial long over, he no longer had one on retainer. There hadn't been a need for it. He'd even thrown the guy's phone number away, not expecting to have use of him again. He could send the attorney a letter through snail mail, but that would take forever, and even if he could get ahold of him, he didn't have the funds available to put him back on retainer.

Off the top of his head, the only thing he could think to do was put in a request form to make an appointment with one of the prison's counselors and hope they could help. If he were lucky, a supervising lieutenant could get him in with a counselor sooner, but if not, it could be another week before he spoke to someone. With a week having already slipped by before he'd received the letter, tracking her would prove difficult, but if he had to wait *another* week? He may never see his son again.

The only limitation Michelle had was money. Did she have enough saved up to travel far? In her letter, she had mentioned not having money to pay the rent, but that didn't mean she hadn't set aside emergency cash for a situation like this. Murphy thought that might be the case, because this didn't seem like a spur-of-the-moment decision, and he knew his wife wasn't an impulsive woman. No, she had to have been plotting this, or at the very least if she didn't have an entire plan ready to go, she had the bones of one in place. Something to get her started that would allow her to hammer out the details as things progressed.

His head swam. Suddenly he was sweating bullets. The urge to vomit was difficult to suppress. Jack hammering behind his ribcage, his heart threatened to burst from within. His chest felt heavy and had tightened up so much he gasped for air, hyperventilating. Murphy dropped to the floor, flat on his ass with his head between his legs, arms resting on his knees. Was he dying? The dam burst and tears streamed from his eyes. He tried to keep the display of emotion in check, but failed. He knew if he were to be caught crying in his cell, it would make him ripe for the picking. Being caught in such an emotionally compromised state would see him branded a bitch, and from that point, it was only a matter of time before the violent, sexual predators of Glenwood paid him a visit. There were plenty of them around, guys who'd been locked up for so long. All they saw was a hole to fuck. If you happened to be the owner of that hole, you could either play ball or you were in for the fight of your life.

It had happened to him once already. If this got out, too, he was fucked.

A fat, bald, tattooed man had been standing outside of Murphy's cell, watching as he lost control. He observed in silence, and as Murphy snapped out of it, he cracked the cell door open and tossed a small object into the cell. The item hit Murphy in the head, snapping him back to reality, anchoring him in the present. Surprised, he scanned the floor. At first, nothing seemed to jump out at him, but then his eyes settled on a white object on the floor. Something that hadn't been in his cell a few moments ago.

Murphy knew what it was the moment his eyes crawled over it

A mark. Small tokens, carved in the shape of a swastika from a Domino game piece.

Reese used them to place a hit on his enemies, or people who'd crossed someone with enough money to pay Reese and his men to do the dirty work.

When delivered a mark, the receiving individual had two options: Carry out the hit, or find your name attached to the next mark. One week to complete the task, no excuses.

"Darius Lewis," said the man known to the inmates of Glenwood as Bic—a name he'd earned when one of the officers who'd taken him out on a hospital trip discovered a lighter in Bic's asshole when returning from the furlough.

"No," Murphy whispered, but Bic hadn't heard, or didn't care. Either way, it didn't matter. Marks were final.

Murphy couldn't kill Lewis, didn't have it in him. Even in a place like this, he still had honor. Friendship meant something to him and he wouldn't sway, even with his life in the balance. In a facility where Darwinism was a way of life, the friendship that had made him stronger also put his life at risk. The fact that Lewis had been chosen as the mark and Murphy tasked to complete the deed was no coincidence. It had to be payback; it was the only thing that made sense.

Payback for befriending a black man rather than siding with the skinheads. Payback for beating the shit out of one of Reese's lapdogs. Reese had to know that Murphy wouldn't kill his friend. No, this was simply a letter of intent. A way for Reese to let Murphy know his transgressions hadn't been forgotten and his days were numbered. He could fight back, maybe even successfully defend himself and live to fight another day. But locked behind bars, it didn't matter if he stopped an attempt on his life, because the attempts on his life would never stop.

Eventually, the reaper would come for him.

There had to be another way. But what? He had to think, come up with a plan. Bartering wouldn't work, Reese had unimpeded access to just about anything he wanted and there wasn't a damn thing on this planet that Murphy could get into the prison that Reese himself wouldn't be able to. Food, drugs, sex, you name it.

Things just kept getting worse. How was he supposed to get Reese off his ass *and* stop his wife from leaving with his son? He wasn't sure he could do either of those things, never mind *both*.

Think, Murphy, think.

The plans!

That was it. Murphy had studied the plans long enough they burned into his brain, and while he couldn't stop Reese from coming after him, escaping Glenwood meant escaping Reese. *And* if he was lucky, he could find a way to stop Michelle from taking his son. By no means did being rid of Glenwood mean that he'd be able to track his wife down or stop her from calling the cops even if he did, but it was a foot in the door. If he could find her, maybe he could appeal to her senses.

She wanted an escape from her current life. Maybe they could escape the country as a family. Flee to somewhere where nobody knew their names. Where nobody would be searching for them. Murphy remembered a story about a woman accused of killing a cyclist who'd fled to Costa Rica and, for a while, had gone undetected. Murphy wasn't anywhere near as high profile as that case. Maybe they could remain hidden and start over again as a family.

But that was something to think about later. First things first. He needed to get the fuck out of prison.

Murphy knew he would need to speak to Lewis about this, get him on board. Now that they were rooming together, it would be impossible to accomplish without involving Lewis. It's not like his friend could claim ignorance to a tunnel in his cell once a staff member discovered Murphy missing. And on a selfish but practical note, Lewis held a job in Glenwood's industrial work area, meaning he had access to tools and equipment that would make tunneling through the floor far easier than doing the work with a spoon or some other primitive object.

Murphy sighed; he didn't like his options. If any of the *many* moving parts of the plan forming in his mind failed to come together, he was as good as dead.

CHAPTER NINE

All week, everything went smoothly and according to plan, though the act of tunneling through a secure facility like Glenwood was both physically taxing, and time consuming. Their secret project was coming down to the wire. Luckily, Lewis had agreed to become a co-conspirator alongside Murphy, because without his help, it would have been impossible to do in a week. Even with his help, they'd barely make it. Murphy never really doubted his friend would leave him hanging, and there were two main reasons. First, Lewis was a ride or die friend and even when their friendship had seemed as if it had evaporated, it had only been because Lewis was trying to keep Murphy out of Reese's crosshairs. Second, if Lewis refused to help, both men were as good as dead. Better to take the risk and fail than to do nothing and be murdered. At least if they were unsuccessful, they'd most certainly be moved to a new, higher security facility, one where Reese's influence held no weight.

Lewis' contributions to the cause were invaluable. His job in the industries department, and his reputation for being a good, trustworthy inmate worker, meant that not only did he have access to tools which could aid the escape, but he generally avoided suspicion of staff members. They were simply too busy, and too complacent to notice a few missing items, and by the time that someone eventually *did* do the job correctly and conduct a proper visual inventory, Murphy and Lewis should be long gone.

The two men had worked tirelessly since the first evening they discussed the plan, scraping away at the cement around the toilet day and night, only stopping at the various times of the day they knew an officer would walk around. For staff, complacency kills, but for inmates, it made their lives a whole hell of a lot easier.

All of this hard work could be destroyed in an instant. It would only take a simple cell search to discover what the two had been up to. But luckily for them, this was another area where the department's staffing crisis played into their hands. It had been years since the staff members of Glenwood had conducted a detailed search of an entire housing unit. The act of searching one such unit was both time and labor intensive and required a full complement of staff. A luxury that Glenwood, like most law enforcement agencies in America, no longer had. These days, the staff were so burnt out from mandatory overtime you were more likely to catch them sleeping on the job than searching a cell. Murphy knew as long as they kept their noses clean and did nothing to draw unnecessary attention to themselves, the chances of someone discovering their little project were as likely as Jesus Christ appearing in the middle of the weight pit in the yard.

Still, one couldn't be too careful, so without divulging what they were up to, they paid a few of the more trustworthy inmates to keep an eye out and give warning if any staff or inmates were getting too close for comfort.

Day six and the coast remained clear.

On the eve before their deadline, the two men finally scraped through the last bit of concrete holding the toilet in place.

They tossed their tools aside and sat there for a moment, neither man ready to break the silence, worried that speaking about it would jinx the operation. Everything hinged on what Murphy had seen on the map. If his interpretation of the plans in relation to the current facility were correct, after removing the large, steel toilet housing, they should be able to drop into what had been bowels of the old facility. If Murphy was wrong, and the plans had simply been the hallucinations of a man's mind stretched to the breaking point, or if the basement were otherwise inaccessible from where they'd dug the tunnel, they were dead men walking.

As if on cue, Murphy and Lewis stood up and took position on each side of the toilet. They looked each other in the eye and nodded when ready, lifting the toilet and moving it, careful not to slide it—the last thing they needed was the obnoxious sound of metal dragging across the floor to alert someone this late in the game.

With the toilet out of the way, Lewis handed Murphy the flashlight he'd stolen. "Let's hope this works, brother. For both of our sakes."

Murphy closed his eyes and said a silent prayer. He'd once heard someone say *there are no atheists in a foxhole*, and since getting locked up, he'd discovered prison was much the same. All of a sudden rapists, murderers, drug dealers were devout religious practitioners. They walked around the building wearing kufis, yamakas, and rosary beads. Men who were the worst of the worst, monsters who'd never given a second thought to a higher power, now converted, worshipping with every fiber of their being—their immortal soul. All within the view of staff, of course. Because most of the newly converted behind bars had had a change of heart for one of two reasons—they'd committed a crime so heinous society couldn't forgive, and now sought forgiveness from a divine entity, or simply because federal laws mandated inmates must be allowed to practice religion, which ultimately led to inmates receiving special religious meals at certain times of the year, depending on what faith they were currently subscribed to. But when those men were released from prison, the sudden discovery of religion disappeared as quickly as it had come about, much the same as soldiers when they returned from an overseas deployment.

There were many gods for a hopeless man to choose from. But when that man's sentence was up and salvation was no longer vital to their sense of self preservation, they cast aside their god of choice. Forgotten, like their victims.

For the entirety of his time behind bars, Murphy had resisted the temptation to seek a higher power, laughed at the men who clearly didn't believe but maintained a facade.

Until now.

His life was on the line, and if there was a deity in existence who could nudge the odds in his favor, he'd sure as shit like to have them on his side.

He opened his eyes and exhaled. He'd been holding his breath for so long without realizing it that his head swam. The anticipation was too much and the vein above his temple throbbed in tandem with the jack-hammering of his heart against its ribcage prison. A wave of nausea washed over him, and his balls felt as if they'd ascended into his abdomen. Shaking the feeling off, he forced himself to act.

Murphy shined the flashlight into the brand-new hole created by the absence of the toilet. The beam of light sliced through the darkness like a scalpel through eager, waiting flesh. Beyond the plumbing of the toilet, Murphy saw only darkness where the beam wasn't strong enough to illuminate.

Relief overtook the nausea, although he knew they weren't out of the woods yet, not by a long shot. Still, that there appeared to be some sort of drop meant there was *something* underneath the floor of the prison. The real test was still before them. If things continued to go smoothly, Glenwood Corrections would soon be a thing of the past, putting

Murphy one step closer to his son, and many, many steps away from Reese and impending homicide.

He tossed aside any remaining doubts, not because he genuinely believed success was now a given, but because a man at the end of his rope would seize any opportunity to cling to hope.

"Jesus Christ, bro, you were right," Lewis said, laughing as he spoke. In the face of the impossible, he broke into hysterics.

"You doubted me?" Murphy said.

"I mean, I believed you thought you saw something. I knew O'Rourke, and I know this place is haunted by its past. I believe in ghosts, and paranormal shit like that. But I guess part of me wasn't convinced, especially when you started talking about plans for the old facility appearing and disappearing. It seemed to me like the hallucinations of a man who's mind was on the brink of collapse, like your brain had created a fantasy in order to protect itself and hold on to whatever sanity remained."

"Really? Are you fucking serious, man? When did you become a therapist?"

Lewis laughed again. "Since I've been watching Dr. Phil every day in this bitch. But seriously, I don't think it would be unrealistic for anyone to assume that staying locked up in segregation took a toll on your mental health man. You did a lot of time down there, and that's not even taking into account all the other shit you've had going on with parole and your family. A man can only take so much, and I know you compartmentalize your problems instead of dealing with them. Eventually, that pressure is going to cause something to snap. I had a friend who'd served in the military, went overseas and saw some shit. When he came home, he never talked about it. One day, he decided enough was enough and suck started his AR15. I don't think you're suicidal or anything like that, but I think maybe you were getting close to your breaking point, and part of that story was a coping mechanism. Clearly, I couldn't have been anymore fucking wrong though, and this tunnel is going to save our lives."

"Yeah, maybe..." Murphy trailed off. He thought he'd heard something, but couldn't be sure.

"What do you mean, maybe? This is it. Once we get out of here, we just have to keep a low profile, make sure we don't get picked up again. Law enforcement all over the country are going to have our pictures, but if we can avoid pigs we're fucking fee, man."

Murphy shook his head and spoke quickly. He was getting nervous, sitting around with a newly dug hole fresh inside of the cell. "That's not what I mean. That last night I was in segregation. When I saw O'Rourke, he said something odd. 'What's the toll on a route paved in blood?' or something like that. I forgot about it at the time, but lying in my bunk last night, it popped into my head out of nowhere, and I've been thinking about it ever since. Thinking about that, and about the entire situation. Why me, Lewis? Why now? This area has been abandoned underneath the prison for how long? And O'Rourke and the plans suddenly materialize after all the time? I couldn't be the first person to have flipped through that book. It doesn't make any sense. I don't know something about the way he emphasized all the shit about evil and latching on to people and places. It sounds fucking nuts, but I'm not gonna lie, that evil never dying, and the Maniac of D Block has got my skin crawling just thinking about it all again. This whole situation is like some shit out of a cheesy 80s horror movie."

Lewis chewed his lip. "Who knows, man? All of this seems too good to be true, but what choice do we have? The time to worry about all of that shit is long gone. We just tunneled through our fucking toilet. Even if we said, 'fuck it' and changed our minds, we've passed the point of no return. Someone is going to find this tunnel, eventually. It might take some time, but someone *will* notice, and when they do, we're absolutely fucked. *And* that's if we aren't already dead by the time someone discovers it. I don't think Reese is going to take his time proving his point with us. A guy like that is gonna want to make an example. I'll take my chance in the tunnel. What's the worst that could happen? We've got some food, we've got tools in case we need to dig some more, and we've got these," Lewis said, holding up a toothbrush with a razor blade melted to the tip. "You ever see what these do to someone's face? Any officer finds us and they're gonna need a plastic surgeon to fix them up. And if Lee Harris really is down there somehow, he's gonna wish he'd stayed dead in the riot."

Murphy nodded his head. Lewis hadn't calmed his fears, but he was right about one thing—they didn't have any other options. "Yeah, you're right. Is everything set for tomorrow? You took care of the arrangement with Ruiz?"

"Sure did. Ruiz has the hots for one of my girls, Trixie, so I had a little talk with him, and in exchange for a diversion Trixie has been sucking him off in the back of the law library for the past few days."

Lewis had been running a pimping operation out of Glenwood for a few years now. He was a savvy businessman and saw an opportunity to make money off sex in the facility. He offered protection to the gay and trans inmates who'd otherwise have been targeted in the facility. The men and women employed by Lewis were happy to work for him—better for the sex to be a choice they made under more favorable terms than to left beaten and abused, possibly killed.

Murphy laughed. "Offering them protection and pimping them out turned out to be a smart move, man. All that money you made, and now this, I wish I had your business sense."

"A day late and a dollar short, man. So, here's the plan.

Tomorrow, Trixie is going to gobble the tube steak one last time, making our part of the bargain with Ruiz paid off. Once Ruiz shoots his load off, he's going to start a fire in the library. The aim is for that happen right around the time the education movement is going on. There's going to be so many inmates roaming around the building at that time, the entire place will be absolute fucking chaos. Plus, that early in the morning, most of the officers haven't gotten around to making sure everyone's cell doors are shut, so when all the staff goes running off with fire extinguishers and they're busy taking care of that whole situation, it's not going to look out of the ordinary for us to be going in and out of our cell. It's almost a guarantee that anyone monitoring the surveillance system is going to be too busy watching the action to notice what is going on in the housing units."

"I like where this is going," Murphy said.

Lewis clapped Murphy's shoulder. "I told you we'd be all set. By the time the officer gets back on post, we should have at least a twenty-minute lead, maybe more. I figure there are three ways this thing could go once he's here again. The first, someone rats us out. There are plenty of snitches around, and I'd be surprised if *nobody* saw us. The second, whatever officer working the area tomorrow, is a go-getter and decides to make a tour around the block after he returns from responding to the fire. I think this is the most likely scenario, especially if they end up calling an emergency count after the fire is taken care of. The third, and best-case scenario, whatever officer works this area tomorrow returns from responding to the fire and then parks his ass at the table and doesn't move until the *routine* morning count. Personally, I'm not counting on this happening, I think it's always best to plan for the absolute worse, and if it ends up being easier than anticipated, well then, we have something else to celebrate when we're on the other side."

Murphy let out a long sigh. He clapped his hands once

and rubbed them together, psyching himself up. "Alright man, looks like there's nothing left to do but wait. Let's cover this hole up until the morning. We've already sat here way too long, bullshitting. Lucky for us, most of the staff around here likes to sleep at night instead of doing their jobs."

They grabbed the toilet and positioned it back in place, once again taking care to avoid scraping it across the floor.

Both men had been locked up for years, had spent plenty of time *waiting*, but with their freedom, and lives in the balance, it would be the longest wait of their lives.

CHAPTER TEN

The next morning after shift change, the cell doors opened promptly at 7:30 A.M. Glenwood corrections, despite all of its current problems, still kept a tight schedule. Although many of the inmates incarcerated at Glenwood were some of the worst behaved prisoners the facility had ever seen, and what little staff currently employed were simultaneously the least disciplined, and the most overworked officers to ever put on the badge, the daily schedule was one thing that operated like clockwork.

Coincidently, all of those things combined formed a perfect storm of conditions to plot and execute a successful prison break.

Shortly after the cell doors opened, their housing unit was summoned to chow. Both Murphy and Lewis made their way to the dining room. Neither man wanted to eat—nerves kept their hunger at bay—but they knew to make an escape attempt without first fueling their bodies would be foolish. It was a risk, leaving the cell for so much time, anyone could happen upon the tunnel they'd made, but neither man knew when their next meal would come and even if things went off without a hitch, it could be days before they were able to stop and rest long enough to eat something more than a quick snack.

By the time they finished eating breakfast and made their way back to the block, there was less than an hour remaining before their expected go time. There was nothing left to do but wait for the fire alert to be called over the intercom.

Officer Manning was in charge of the area this morning, a perfect hit as far as they were concerned. Manning was about as lazy as they come and didn't give a shit what went on so long as the inmates in his area weren't fighting. Most of the time, he didn't even bother touring his area. He simply sat in the large, safety glass enclosure overlooking the module, stuffing his face with McDonald's breakfast sandwiches, washing them down with Ghost Energy drinks. Between the horrible diet, overconsumption of caffeine, and morbidly obese frame, he was a cardiac event waiting to happen. The same reasons Manning was a prime heart attack candidate also made Murphy and Lewis confident there was no chance he'd stumble across the hole before they jumped down it. They were looking at a few hours of lead time before being discovered, much better than the 20 minutes they were planning for.

Sadly, staff like Manning were no longer the exception. They were the rule. Since the old facility burned down it had become normal for officers to monitor the housing units from the control area, rather than from within the unit itself. There had been a time, years ago, when officers were required to remain in the housing units, and were even held liable in civil lawsuits put forth by inmates after getting into fights if it was discovered the fight happened and the officer *wasn't* in the unit. But when staffing became a crisis and Glenwood became a more dangerous place for both inmates and officers, the administrators changed the policy in order to keep workers' compensation claims to a minimum. Worker's compensation claims were a thorn in the warden's side and were another reason it was impossible to maintain a full complement of staff.

The result was a prison where officers spent less time on workers' compensation but did less work and were no longer on the hook for civil suits.

The same policy change was a large part of the reason Glenwood inmates had free rein of the facility, and the reason a plot such as the one Murphy and Lewis had concocted was even a possibility.

Murphy and Lewis sat at a table playing chess, waiting for the alarm to sound. Though there was nothing out of the ordinary going on at the moment, the housing area was so loud that Murphy had trouble concentrating on his next move. One hundred men congregated in an indoor space, carrying on dozens of separate conversations meant that even when things were quiet, they weren't really *quiet*. But if the room were dead silent, Murphy didn't think he'd be able to concentrate, anyway. His mind kept hopping to the various conversations happening around him, trying to pick out any sign that their secret had been discovered. So far, it didn't seem as if anyone was talking about it, but that didn't mean nobody knew. There were plenty of rats running around Glenwood, and not all of them had tails.

Murphy was dressed for comfort and ease of mobility. He wore his black, state issued recreation sweatpants and a white t-shirt along with a pair of brown workbooks. Initially, he was going to wear sneakers, in case they needed to move quickly and quietly, but Lewis had convinced him otherwise. They were headed into an unknown underground area. A waterproof, heavy-duty boot made more sense than a thin sneaker protecting their feet.

Inside the housing unit, the temperature was bearable, if not comfortable. Often during the warmest months of the year, the module would become so humid the floors were soaked in water like a slip and slide. Officers had been known to go out on injury from slipping on the floor before they ever got a chance to break up the fight they were running to in the first place. Not today, though.

Today, the air conditioning was working as intended. Despite that, sweat trickled down Murphy's forehead, along his back, and down the crack of his ass. It was still early, yet his shirt was saturated with sweat. He fidgeted around, not only trying to get comfortable but also trying to remove the wedgie plaguing him without having to pick his ass in front of everyone. Murphy thanked God that there were no staff around at the moment because the amount of perspiration leaking from his pores made him look guilty as sin.

Lewis moved a piece across the board. "Relax man."

"I am relaxed."

"Yeah? Because your shirt would get you first place in a wet t-shirt contest. You're sweating like a hooker in church."

"I'm as calm as I'm gonna get, man. I'm just ready to get this thing started. What the fuck is taking Ruiz so long?"

"Chill, it's still early. He's gonna do it right when they call the movements, which should be," Lewis looked at his watch, "any minute now."

As if on cue, the crackle of the overhead speaker cut Lewis off.

Code red in the library. Code red in the library. All staff respond to the library for a code red. Glenwood fire department notified and en route.

Murphy remained seated at the table and watched as officer Manning opened the control center door and took off running with a fire extinguisher as fast as his enormous frame could carry him, looking every bit like a soup sandwich on his way out the door.

With a bit of luck, the fire would be a good one and it would be a while before Manning returned. He hoped that the fire department already on the way meant the blaze was a good one.

The instant officer Manning left the area and was no longer in sight, a calm washed over Murphy, forcing his nervousness aside. It happened the same way before he killed the monster who'd ruined his son, nothing but nerves until go time, and then it was like someone flicked a switch.

Once again, it was go time.

They abandoned their chess game and made their way to the cell, trying to look as normal as possible. Murphy was eager to get going and could hardly contain himself. He knew Lewis had to be feeling the same. How could he not? Still, they kept themselves in check, making it a point to mask their eagerness and walk, rather than run. This close to the finish line, there was no need to draw unwanted attention to themselves.

They reached the cell, crossed the threshold, and closed the door behind them.

Neither man had seen Reese stick a paper towel in the locking mechanism earlier to prevent it from catching. And *had* they been paying closer attention to their surroundings, rather than trying to play it cool, they might have seen Reese and two of his cronies watching them like hawks circling prey.

By the time Murphy and Lewis closed the door, the three skinheads were already crossing the housing module, rapidly closing the distance between them and their prey.

Reese stood against the wall with one foot up, flat against the surface. His arms were crossed over his chest, hands clenching his prison jumper. He watched from afar as Murphy and Lewis sat at a table playing chess. The sight alone causing the blood to boil in his veins. He couldn't believe the nerve of that piece of shit Murphy. How dare he spit in the face of his white brothers in the joint? Clearly, he hadn't gotten his point across, but what else could he have done? He'd already taken Murphy in every way a man could take another man, and yet the fucker still dared to defy him.

Reese wouldn't allow that transgression to go unpunished.

The moment Murphy refused to carry out the mark, he'd signed his own goddamn death warrant. But Reese wasn't going to pass this off to someone else. This was a special occasion, and he was going to take care of both of those pricks. He needed to prove a point. Make sure that *nobody* forgets what happens when you fuck with Jason Reese.

But before that happened, he was going to have some fun. Reese had big plans for those two. If Murphy thought getting his ass taken was bad, he had another thing coming because he was going to be sucking dick like there was no tomorrow. His little fucking buddy's salty load would be the last thing he'd ever taste before Reese's blade ran across his fucking throat and sawed his goddamn head off of his shoulders. And when he was done? Lewis was going to get his own cock-meat sandwich when Reese chopped his pecker off and force fed it to him.

Looking at the two of them, Reese knew they were up to something. Murphy was drenched in sweat and fidgeting like a tweaker. Lewis whispered something to his friend and Murphy quickly settled down.

Yeah, those two fucks were up to something. Maybe he'd get a chance to handle these two counts sooner than he'd anticipated.

He called over Bic and Kelly—two members of the gang who were always up for dirty work—and ran them through the idea that had been marinating in his brain. They were going to get those two ball bags cornered in a cell and take care of them for good.

Reese grabbed a small stack of paper towels and wadded them up. While the two cornballs sat at the table looking suspicious as hell despite their efforts to play it cool, Reese used their lack of situational awareness to his advantage and stuck the wad into locking mechanism before making his way back to his cronies. Now he simply needed to wait for them to enter the room and close the door. It would shut, but the lock wouldn't engage. As long as they didn't slam it shut hard enough for it to swing back open, they'd never be the wiser.

Then Reese and his boys would make their move.

He continued to observe the two men, silently stewing in his hatred. Beside him, his two cronies kept silent as well. They knew better than to chum the waters when the shark was hungry.

Suddenly, the crackle of a loudspeaker cut through the silence, announcing a fire in the library. All the inmates in the area paused to listen, but as the fire was nowhere near the housing module, they quickly went about their business as if nothing had happened.

Everyone except Murphy and Lewis, both of whom walked straight to their cell the moment officer Manning was no longer on his post.

Gotcha, Reese thought.

"Let's go," he said. The two overgrown lapdogs followed their pack leader. Reese didn't know what those two were up to, but it had to be a major. Their poker faces gave them away, and if officer Manning wasn't such a shit bag, he'd have noticed their behavior right away. Besides, the timing of the fire and their immediate response to it was too big of a coincidence, and Reese didn't believe in such things.

Whatever the two of them were up to, he didn't give a flying fuck. All he knew was that their little scheme had tossed them right in his lap.

Reese and the gang stopped in front of the cell door. "You

boys ready for this? They don't leave this cell alive; you understand me?" The skinheads nodded.

Reese swung the door open and said, "Surprise, you cock…"

The cell was empty. Murphy and Lewis had pulled a disappearing act, literally. The toilet no longer sat against the wall, but in the middle of the cell.

Where the toilet had once been—a hole.

"They're not getting away from me that easily. Once we kill those fuckers, the warden will thank us for cleaning up this mess," Reese said.

CHAPTER ELEVEN

Murphy stood up and straightened his shirt. He'd underestimated the distance to the ground and landed wrong, falling flat on his face in the process. Still, he'd been luckier than Lewis, who was now hobbling around in the dark like a wounded animal. If Lewis hadn't had the foresight to throw their mattress down first to create a landing pad, they might have both been fucked. If Lewis couldn't shake off whatever was wrong, they still might be.

"Hey man, are you alright?" Murphy asked.

"Yeah, I think so. I tweaked something, but I think I can walk it off. I don't think it's broken."

Murphy shook his head. "Fuck. Ok whatever you do, don't take your boot off. If you do that, it could swell up and then you're not going to be able to get it back on. We'll take it as slow as we can for the time being. That way, we can get our bearings straight and hopefully you'll be able to move quicker once we figure out where we are going. If we're lucky, nobody is gonna realize we're missing until we are long gone."

Lewis sucked his teeth. "What do you mean 'Once we

figure out where we're going,' I thought you memorized the layout?"

"I did, but I've never been down here before. Have you ever seen blueprints? I'm not a fucking engineer man. Now imagine those blueprints were drawn by hand on an old, weathered piece of paper that was crinkled up and looked like it had been hidden in someone's asshole for two decades. And it's dark as hell down here man, that flashlight is a piece of shit. You couldn't have stolen one that works?"

"I didn't see you risking your ass stealing any of the equipment. That's the best I could do, so if you don't like it, feel free to get fucked."

Both men were stressed and were starting to take it out on each other.

Murray sighed. "Just chill out. I'll get us out of here. We can't be at each other's throats now. We're too close to the finish line. Getting out of here is gonna be the straightforward part. Not getting caught is gonna be the problem we need to solve. We never game-planned that far out."

"No, but we were working on a short timeline. There wasn't much in the way of choices. It was either escape or get murdered."

Murphy nodded. "Yeah, well, it's a little late in the game for that. We'll cross that bridge when we get the fuck out of here. Let's just keep moving. If you need to rest, I'll stop, but being down here gives me the willies. I can't get O'Rourke and The Maniac out of my head."

"Then let's just go. Don't worry about me, I'll be fine."

Murphy scanned the underground area with the afore-mentioned shitty flashlight. It was tough to tell exactly where they were, but Murphy thought they were in the mechanical room that had been marked on the plans. If he remembered correctly, there was some sort of tunnel at one end of the sizable area that connected with a smaller passageway which spilled out underneath a highway overpass. It wasn't exactly a sewer, but it was the closest comparison Murphy could think of.

Overhead, water dripped from the ceiling, plinking off the ground. The surrounding walls were crumbling, and the stench of rot and mildew permeated the air. It was clear this area had been derelict for a long time. Who knew how long? Decades? By the looks of things, it was entirely possible nobody had set foot down here since the fire. None of the equipment seemed to be functional, and why would it? If they simply built a new foundation over the old basement, surely the power would have been disconnected. The water dripping from the pipes overhead led Murphy to believe the only thing still functioning were the PVC pipes from the toilets and sinks in the cells above.

The two men walked the room slowly, searching for anything that may be of use while also taking care to navigate through the rubble of the past. Piles of cement and stone littered the area, along with overturned shelves and even old metal bunk beds. After a short while Murphy eye's adjusted to the lack of light. In the distance, he thought he saw where the mechanical room spilled into the drainage tunnels.

"Look over there. You see that? That's where we need to go," Murphy said before sprinting to the end of the room. In his excitement, he'd forgotten about Lewis' injury, leaving his friend limping behind. Coming up on the tunnel, Murphy cartoonishly skidded to a halt, his feet slipping on the loose rocks beneath them.

Fear and anger fought for control over his emotions when he realized what he was looking at. A large fence which spanned the archway and climbed from floor to ceiling blocked the tunnel off. A heavy-duty lock kept it secured.

"Fuck!" Murphy yelled. "Lewis, it's fucking locked! You got anything on you to smash this?"

Lewis hobbled over, still trailing a good distance behind Murphy. His ankle clearly bothered him more than he was willing to admit. Shaking his head, he replied, "Nothing heavy enough to break that."

"Fuck," Murphy said. "Ok, we're gonna have to look around for a big stone or a piece of cement. Something heavy and solid. There's plenty of rubble around here. There's gotta be something big enough to smash the lock."

Lewis picked up a large piece of stone. The edges were jagged and sharp. He turned it about in his hand as he finally reached Murphy, presenting the stone to him with a smile on his face. "This should work."

Murphy grabbed the rough stone, gently tossed it up—the stone barely leaving his palm—before agreeing with Lewis. "Yeah, this should do the trick."

He held the stone over the lock, slowly bringing it up and down, mimicking the arc he'd take to smash it, making sure it lined up just right. The last thing he wanted to do was to crush a finger down here. Finally, when he felt comfortable enough, he raised the stone over his head and brought it down hard. The impact reverberated through his entire arm, a shockwave of concussive force from wrist to shoulder. He even felt a spike of pain in one of his tooth fillings. The stone's jagged edge bit into his palm, drawing blood. Ignoring the pain, he brought the stone up and down, again and again until the lock was bent and twisted. Despite his efforts, the lock held.

"It's no use," Murphy said. "These heavy-duty locks are built so guys like us can't get through them. We need bolt cutters; this isn't going to work. Any ideas?"

Murphy jiggled the lock, hoping maybe it would come undone after the beating he'd delivered to it. After a few moments of fiddling with it, he became annoyed by Lewis' silence and spun around. "Hey man, did you fucking hear me?"

Murphy's jaw dropped, as did the stone he was holding. Lewis had been unable to respond because one of the skinheads—a guy nicknamed Bic—stood behind Lewis, holding him with one large arm across the forehead and face. In the man's other hand was a long, sharp strip of metal. The rusty tip pressed into his friend's neck, dimpling the flesh. A line of blood trickled down his neck. Flanking Bic and his hostage were Reese and Kelly. Reese had the biggest shit-eating grin Murphy had ever seen plastered across his face.

Murphy couldn't believe it. All the meticulous planning they'd done. How could they be so stupid as to allow Reese and his goons to get the drop on them? He'd been too obsessed with breaking the lock open and now it was too late because, barring a miracle, they were as good as dead. Murphy only hoped he'd have an opportunity to do some damage, maybe take one or two of them along for the ride to hell. A 3 on 2 against men the size of the skinheads wasn't a fight they could win. Murphy knew that, but he wanted to make sure they never forgot him.

Reese spoke. "I've gotta say, I didn't see this one coming. I knew you had *something* in you, Murphy. That's why I gave you so many chances to do the right thing. But you had to force my hand, didn't you?" Reese and Kelly both stepped forward. Murphy backed into the heavy fencing. He turned his head side to side, looking for a way out, but the two assailants had already begun fanning out in order to prevent him from making a break in either direction.

"Don't try to run, asshole. You're just going to get your friend killed. Why don't you come on over here and we'll talk this out?"

"Yeah? Now you want to talk. You're gonna kill him no matter what I do. Go fuck yourself, bitch."

Reese laughed. "I'm the bitch? You've got that wrong, buddy. You were the one shitting out my kids after I fucked you, so wouldn't that make you *my* bitch?

Murphy had heard enough. He charged at Reese, but Kelly was ready for it and launched his body at Murphy like a missile, spearing him to the ground before Murphy got anywhere near Reese. The two men hit the ground with a thud, rolling around. Punches flew from both combatants, but none of them landed cleanly. The men were too wrapped up to get any leverage behind the blows.

Reese stalked his way over to the two inmates scuffling like school children and picked Murphy up by the collar of his shirt, punching him in the gut with his free hand. Spit flew from his mouth as the oxygen was forced from his lungs.

Murphy was winded from the blow, but it was a life-or-death situation and the dog in him refused to quit. Murphy lashed out in retaliation but with the wind knocked out of him, all the pop had been taken out of his own feeble counterattack.

Reese responded with another strike of his own, this time a vicious head butt that shattered Murphy's nose, flattening it like a pancake and spraying crimson syrup all over both men.

Murphy choked on his blood, coughing globs of snot and plasma up. Reese dragged him to where Bic held Lewis's hostage and forced him to his knees. "Pull his pants down, Kelly. Since these two love to mix race so much, we're gonna let them have some inter-racial right now."

Kelly's face went slack. "What?"

Reese stared at Kelly; his eyes were dead serious. "Pull his pants down and fluff him."

"I'm not jerking anyone off, Reese. Are you fucking serious?"

"If you don't do what the fu…"

A geyser of blood erupted from Reese's neck and behind it, a long, black object pierced one side of his neck and protruded from the other.

A river of red poured from the wound, soaking Murphy as a large, hulking behemoth of a man yanked the object, ripping it from Reese's neck.

The lifeless corpse fell on top of Murphy, pinning him to

the ground. A gloved hand wiped the tip of the long, black object—a Monadnock expandable button, the "safety tip" ground down to a jagged point, turning the blunt object into a twenty-one inch heavy-duty, heat-treated steel knife.

The man stood well over six feet tall, massive in both height and frame. A real life giant. Dressed in Glenwood Correctional Institute's signature dark black, military style BDU's, the man dwarfed Arnold Schwarzenegger in his prime. The uniform was tattered and worn, old. Underneath the rips and tears in the cloth, his exposed skin was scarred and burned. In other places, wounds still festered. The man's face was a horrific sight. Poorly healed scars ran from eyebrow to jaw line on both sides of his face. A milky white film covered the only eye in his head. The other eye was gone or covered with scar tissue and melted skin.

Murphy gagged, not from the dead body on top of him, but the smell wafting off the giant. Mildew and decay assaulted his nostrils. Grave rot mixed in, making a menagerie of putrid smells.

"Jesus Christ, it's fucking Lee Harris," Lewis said.

The sudden intrusion of Lewis' voice snapped Bic out of the trance he'd been in. He shoved Lewis away and devoted his full attention to The Maniac of D block. "I don't know any Lee Harris, but this fucker right here is a dead man. Let's get that son of a bitch, Kelly."

Kelly and Bic launched a joint attack at The Maniac. Bic dove at him, but The Maniac caught him mid-flight and tossed him like a rag doll. Bic's colossal frame sailed through the air and collided with the steel fence that had been blocking the tunnel with enough force to knock the fencing down. It clattered to the ground and Bic landed with a thud and a grunt on top of the steel fencing.

Lewis turned his attention to his friend and tried rolling Reese's bloody corpse off of Murphy, but the man was too large, his dead weight far too heavy. "You're gonna have to help me out here, man."

Murphy grunted as he worked in tandem with Lewis to shove Reese off of him. The two pushed with all their might and managed to free Murphy. Lewis grabbed his friend under the arms and tried to help him up, but Murphy shoved his hands away. He didn't need help getting up; he needed to get the fuck out of dodge while they preoccupied The Maniac with their uninvited company.

"Look, the fence is busted. This is our chance," Murphy said.

"Alright, let's go."

Behind The Maniac, Kelly saw the blurry forms of Murphy and Lewis as they took off running like the little pussies they were. He ignored them as he kept his focus on the abomination Lewis identified as Lee Harris, as if that name was supposed to have some kind of significance. The two chicken-shits he'd deal with after he slaughtered the mother fucker who' done Reese in.

The Maniac stood as still as a statue as Kelly Maneuvered forward, closing the gap while slashing wildly in front of him with the shank that Bic had dropped when The Maniac tossed him aside.

Vacancy. That's what Kelly saw in the eyes of The Maniac as he approached, as if the thought of getting diced to ribbons by a shank was nothing to be worried about. If he cared, he made no indication, didn't budge an inch as Kelly approached.

When he was within an arm's distance, Kelly sliced again, this time the shank being met with resistance as it cut through

The Maniac's correction officer uniform, parting the skin beneath it. Fetid, black sludge cascaded from lips of the wound. The Maniac looked down at the muck spilling from his body with indifference. He made no sound when the shank had opened him, nor did he make even the slightest expression of pain. It was as if the man felt nothing as his skin was ripped open.

Kelly continued carving The Maniac, Lee Harris, like a rotisserie chicken to no effect. He grunted with each swipe, putting all his effort into it. He hadn't known that slashing a human body repeatedly was so tiring. His lungs burned and his arms ached with each swipe. If it weren't for the black ooze flying through the air, splattering the floor and covering Kelly's face he'd have been questioning if he were actually cutting the man.

While Kelly sliced and diced, he noticed Bic rise to his feet and creep up behind The Maniac. Bic wrapped his arms around the man's tank-like frame and squeezed. The veins in his head and arms bulged as he struggled to control The Maniac. Kelly knew there was no way his friend would be able to keep hold of the giant for more than a few seconds.

"Kill this motherfucker!" Bic shouted.

"I'm working on it!"

With Bic struggling to maintain the bearhug grip, Kelly jabbed the shank into The Maniac, thrusting it forward and pulling it back again and again. It felt good to stick that fucker. Felt good to poke him for Reese.

"Don't stop!" Bic said.

And Kelly *didn't* stop, couldn't have stopped even if he'd wanted to. He was a man possessed, lost in the music of violence, dancing to a tune that only men who'd done violence recognized. There was no drum beat to follow, the rhythm of this tune was the wet squelching noises echoing through the dark room with each thrust of the shank as Kelly stabbed again and again. The putrid stench of the vile, black substance coursing through The Maniac's veins made Kelly gag, but still he continued the assault. Reese would be avenged at all costs. But as Kelly's arms grew tired, and each breath became increasingly difficult to take, his vicious attack slowed considerably. He looked every bit the lunatic he'd become when overtaken by the violent spell—arms, face, and chest, all covered in the black sludge.

"What the fuck are you?" Bic said, the tremor in his voice reinforcing Kelly's knowledge the assault had born no fruit.

The Maniac remained stoic, silent, the blank visage of his face etched forever among the scarred and charred flesh.

Kelly mustered all his strength and pulled the shank back once more. Bic screamed, "Die Fucker!" as Kelly rammed it forward, but The Maniac spun around at the last minute. The shank plunged into Bic's back, flesh parting like warm butter as the tip pierced his skin until it had sunk deep, puncturing his lung. Blood pooled around the handle and ran along Kelly's, coating it in his friend's warm, red essence.

The moment the shank pierced Bic's flesh, The Maniac sprang into action, no longer content to take everything Kelly dished out. He pumped his legs backward, pushing his two opponents into a stone pillar with enough force debris and chunks of stone to break loose, clattering around them. One such hunk of stone crashed on top of Kelly's skull, and, after a sharp pain, he felt nothing more.

He collapsed to the ground like a sack of potatoes. A large wound appeared in the place where the stone had collided with his head. Blood rushed from his broken skull and through the fragments of bone. His exposed brain seemed to pulsate as his body gave out.

Kelly's grip on the shank remained true even as his body collapsed. The force of his falling body pulled the shank down and out, tearing Bic's flesh as he fell to the ground next to Kelly.

The Maniac stomped Bic's skull like a child squashing

bugs. His eyes popped from his skull as his head crumpled. Blood rivers ran from his ears. The Maniac continued stomping. Brain matter squirted from the ruined head like a Gushers fruit snack.

The Maniac grabbed the shank that had been used on him and shoved it into Kelly's face. He was already dead, but it didn't stop Lee Harris from sticking Kelly's eyeball like a pig, piercing the orb. Gooey ocular fluid squirted from the wound. Lee Harris didn't care that both men were dead. He continued stabbing and slashing the dead man's body and face with the same reckless abandon Kelly had used on him earlier. Kelly's DNA painted the surrounding area. Blood spray coated the walls, ran down the stone pillars and pooled around his mauled frame.

One last time, he jabbed the metal into Kelly's chest, hitting the breastbone. The tip of the shank snapped off and at last The Maniac was finished. He tossed the broken weapon aside, shoved both of his hands into one of the larger punctures in Kelly's chest. He twisted and wriggled his hands until they were wrist deep in the cavity, a violent fisting of the wound.

With a grunt, The Maniac pulled Kelly's ribcage apart with a crack and ripped his heart from his chest. He dropped the dead organ to the ground and turned in the direction Lewis and Murphy had fled.

The sounds of violence echoed down the hallway behind Murphy and Lewis as they made their way down the dark tunnel, putting as much distance between Glenwood and Lee Harris as possible. Murphy had no clue what was transpiring, but he had no intention of finding out.

That some sort of undead ghoul really had been waiting in the bowels of Glenwood was a tough pill to swallow, although he had witnessed it with his own two eyes. It was amazing the lengths the human brain will go to in order to protect itself. But he couldn't let his brain tune this one out or deny it. Doing so would surely invite a horrific end.

Glenwood truly was hell. Human violence, atrocities, ghosts, corpses reanimated by some sort of evil presence. Murphy needed to be free and clear of this place. After that, maybe he could spread the word. People had to know about this. Glenwood needed to be leveled, nuked even. A ghoul like The Maniac shouldn't exist, it was an affront to humanity. A real-life killer straight out of a cheesy 80s slasher flick.

Murphy pressed on despite the heaviness in his chest. He blamed the cigarettes for that one, a habit he'd only picked up after getting locked up. He justified the foul addiction in his mind by telling himself it eased his stress, allowed him to pass time and relax in a place where relaxation was seemingly impossible.

Behind him, Lewis stopped running, clearly spent. He wasn't a smoker like Murphy was, but he was older and didn't make an effort to work out the way that Murphy had most of the time he'd been in prison. It was a fantasy of Murphy's to come home "prison jacked" and ravage his wife like they were on their honeymoon again. In his mind, he thought that she'd be excited for him to come home with a chiseled physique, but in truth, she preferred his dad bod, and he was only projecting a childish fantasy onto her.

Murphy went back to Lewis, who was bent over, hands on his thighs.

"I can't keep going man, I'm fucking done," Lewis said.

Murphy grabbed his friend's arm and draped it over his shoulder. "I'm not leaving you here with that fucking lunatic. Put your weight on me and let's fucking go. If it's too much, we can hide until you feel up to moving again."

They hobbled down the hallway, which had been getting steadily wider until it had doubled in size. The water running steadily at their feet told Murphy they were headed in the right direction. Thankfully, because of the width of the corridor, the water wasn't deep, only enough to get the bottom of their shoes wet. The last thing either of them needed was soaking wet feet. It could still be some time before they were able to take their shoes off and relax.

Murphy could feel Lewis still struggling with his injury. He said to Lewis, "Just down this corridor, man, keep going. We're almost there."

Heavy footfalls and splashing water echoed behind the escaping convicts.

"Shit, he's here," Lewis said.

"Just keep going. Look down the tunnel. I think it's getting lighter. That's gotta be the end!"

"Fuck man, we're so close. Don't let him catch up."

As the words escaped his lips, The Maniac's steel baton whipped through the air, the heavy handle whacking Lewis in the back of the head. He dropped to his knee, dazed from the impact.

Lee Harris appeared from the darkness behind them, closing the distance in a few long, quick steps. Logic dictated it should be impossible for a man that size to move as quickly as he had, yet he did. The existence of The Maniac defied logic. Why should anything else about him be dictated by previously held notions about what was or wasn't possible?

Lewis rose to his feet and turned, ready to defend himself, but he wasn't ready for how quickly Harris had reached them. The Maniac scooped up the baton and swung it in a downward, backhanded motion. It cracked Lewis in the face, shattering his cheekbone. Fragments of teeth rained down like candy from a piñata, scattering on the ground. The sharpened tip of the baton had slashed his face, parted flesh and left a window in his mouth made of sinewy strands of skin and meat. Blood poured from the gaping wound as Lewis lay face down on the ground. He coughed blood, and another tooth flew out of his mouth, clinking onto the floor beneath him.

The Maniac raised the baton again, ready to end Lewis. The attack had happened so quickly neither man had seen it coming, but now Murphy was ready to die for his friend. He sprinted as fast as his legs would take him, spearing Harris, but the man was built like a brick shithouse and the attack didn't budge the monster. Murphy had done more harm to himself than anything else. The impact sent a stab of pain through his shoulder, but there was no time to react. Their lives were on the line. Ignoring the pain, he wrapped his arms around Harris and pumped his legs like a piston, trying to take Harris to the ground.

There was a split second where Murphy thought he might take The Maniac to the ground, but the ghoul was too strong and Murphy's grip too weak from the stinger. Harris' feet moved maybe an inch before he planted them in the ground, stopping any momentum Murphy had. He interlocked his hands together, creating a club with his massive mitts, and hammered down between Murphy's shoulder blades. The pain was incredible. The air rushed out of Murphy's lungs. He might as well have been hit with a sledgehammer. He crashed to the ground flat on his face and Harrison raised his leg, quickly stomping down. Murphy's first instinct when hitting the ground was to roll away and create space, an instinct that prevented his brains from being pulped. The enormous boot hit the ground where Murphy had been an instant after he'd moved.

Scrambling to his feet, Murphy took a defensive stance, though he still had trouble lifting his arm from the stinger. The Maniac mauled face remained emotionless. To him, Murphy must be nothing more than a bug to be squashed. Another death to fuel the evil lurking within Glenwood.

Murphy surveyed the area, searching for something, anything, he could use as a weapon. He was smart enough to know he had no chance in hell to win a hand-to-hand fight with the creature who'd taken out Reese, Kelly, and Bic single handedly.

He saw large chunks of stone littering the surrounding ground, but nothing else. Having no other option, Murphy grabbed the largest one within reach and chucked it at Harris. A wave of triumph spread throughout Murphy; his aim was true. He knew it the moment the stone left his hand.

The rock sailed through the air and pelted Harris square on the cheekbone. A sickening crunch echoed through the cave-like depths of the basement. Harris' cheek exploded; the orbital bone destroyed. The monster's eye dangled from its socket. Black, chunky ooze flowed from the gaping wound it The Maniac's face. Maggots wriggled around in the sludgy pool of fluid spreading on the ground. Other than visually observing the physical damage done, there was no indication Murphy had done anything to Harris. The fucker hadn't even flinched.

What would it take to stop this abomination? Could Murphy kill him? Cripple him? He couldn't be sure of either of those things, but one thing Murphy *was* sure of was that if he didn't figure something out quickly, this crypt in the bowels of the prison would be his final resting place.

Out of the corner of his eye, Murphy saw Lewis rise to his feet. If Harris was aware of Lewis, he made no sign. He simply watched Murphy gather a few more large rocks. Maybe death by a thousand stones would do the trick, or at least slow the fucker down. One by one, he chucked everything in the surrounding area that looked as if it would hurt. Rocks, chunks of metal, anything he could find. Most of the projectiles found their mark, but none of it did the physical damage the first stone had, nor did they appear to slow Harris down in the slightest. The Maniac, unfazed, stalked ever closer even as Murphy backpedaled, continuing to throw everything but the kitchen sink. Had there been a ditch sink, Murphy'd have thrown that, too.

While Harris was distracted by—or indifferent to— Murphy's assault, Lewis crept up behind the behemoth. His gaze was trained low, and he moved in step with Harris. At first Murphy had no clue what the hell Lewis was doing, but as he moved closer, Lewis extended his arm toward something strapped to Harris' leg.

A large canister of Sabre Red pepper spray!

There was no way to know if the canister would still work. Who knew how old the thing was? And if it worked, would it be effective against the abomination? Either way, they were out of options. Maybe Lewis would buy them enough time to escape.

Lewis took one more step in tandem with Harris, who was now in striking distance of Murphy, and reached for the canister. For a moment, the velcro on the holster held true before finally releasing. Lewis snatched the canister, but that moment of resistance where the velcro held was all it took to blow Lewis' plan to shit.

Harris turned, and in a lightning quick motion, brought the baton down on Lewis' wrist. There was a sickening snap, like a tree splitting in a hurricane, and Lewis dropped the canister, falling to the ground, clutching his shattered wrist.

Harris picked up the canister and aimed it at Lewis' face. He held it there for a moment before unloading a blast of orange fog into Lewis' wide open, screaming mouth. The spray painted his entire face and chest orange. It entered the micro abrasions on his face and coated his eyeballs.

Murphy, still rolling around on the ground in pain, heard him choke from the intense burning and respiratory reaction the concoction of ten percent oleoresin capsicum caused his friend to experience. The residual spray in the air burned

Murphy and caused him to cough. He could only imagine how his friend felt at that moment.

Lewis rolled around on the floor, screaming and clawing at his face. There would be no departmental policy mandated shower after this use of force. Lewis was getting the full effect.

Harris stood over Lewis and sprayed again, unloading the rest of the canister on Lewis as he continued to scream like a madman. Anyone who'd been hit by OC before knew it caused men to go insane. The itching and burning. The feeling that you couldn't breathe, even though you knew the fact you were talking and screaming, meant you *were* breathing.

Snot, vomit, tears, and blood were everywhere. Harris tossed the empty can aside and removed a set of handcuffs from the pouch on his belt. A quick swipe of the metal hoop with his finger popped the cuffs open with a ratcheting noise that echoed through the tunnel. He clutched the open cuff in his bear paw and swung downward, using the claw-like tip of the cuff to cleave through Lewis' eye. The end hooked through his eyeball and Harris grunted, pushing harder until his untold strength forced the metal through thin bone behind the eyeball, giving Lewis the first ever transorbital lobotomy performed with a set of handcuffs. Lewis' legs jerked violently for a few moments before going stiff. His body slackened; his life essence evaporated.

Lewis was dead.

Murphy witnessed this and scrambled to his feet, the pain in his body miraculously gone with the additional dump of adrenaline that had hit his body. The fight-or-flight response working as biology intended. He said a silent prayer for his friend as his legs carried him away from The Maniac as fast as they were capable of moving him. Right now, there was no time to stop and mourn the loss of his friend. That would need to wait until he escaped from this hellhole, a feat which looked more unlikely with each passing moment.

He understood now what he hadn't before. The evil present in Glenwood had existed long before Glenwood existed. When the riots happened and the place was reduced to rubble, it hadn't dissipated; it had simply latched on to a bad man and lingered within him, transforming the man into a deathless killing machine. Murphy couldn't be sure, but he thought whatever the *evil* was, had dug in its hooks once more; new building be damned. O'Rourke wasn't Casper the Friendly Ghost. He hadn't shown Murphy a way out to help a man at the end of his rope. No, O'Rourke was an extension of the evil present here, a way to ensure the presence was given the fuel it needed—blood and misery.

If he escaped this hellscape, Murphy knew nobody would believe his story. He knew it sounded like horse shit, like the internal ramblings of a man whose brain had gone soft from too much time in segregation with no human interaction. Not long ago Murphy himself thought so. Evil, he had once thought, was tangible. Real. Rooted in humanity. But now he knew the truth: *evil* existed outside the boundaries of humanity as well. Lunacy, the idea that a *place* could be *evil*, but now that it had shown itself, he recognized it for what it was and realized that himself, Lewis, and the rest of the inmates of Glenwood Correctional Institute had been living in a place where *evil* was the norm.

It had been hibernating.

Biding its time.

Growing stronger.

Now it stalked him. Hunter and prey.

Closer to the exit now, the bright, inviting light of freedom cast aside the darkness, vanquishing its enemy as it has since the dawn of time. Murphy's heart raced. From adrenaline and fear, yes, but from hope, too. He'd been locked up for years, his freedom taken from him. Before his stint at Glenwood, he'd never quite understood the beauty of freedom. How could he have understood when, from the moment he'd been born, he had never had to fight for, or otherwise earn, his freedom?

But once that freedom had been ripped away, Murphy served his time, dreaming of an early release. Of the day he'd be free once more. Dreamed of a home cooked meal, of hugging his wife and son. Dreamed of the day when he could wipe his ass behind the privacy of a closed door or go to sleep and not have to hear the moans of another man masturbating on the bunk beneath him. Things you rarely consider until they are no longer a part of your life.

The parole board had ripped those dreams from him when they denied his early release, but here, in the bowels of Glenwood, it reappeared—an actual light at the end of a tunnel.

But just as the light will vanquish the dark, darkness reappears, embracing the world in its cold, empty embrace.

Murphy's hopes were snuffed out, just like the light was each evening. Extinguished with the realization that a massive, grate-like cover stood between him and the outside world, its chain links cruelly exposing an outside world they would not permit him entry to.

Behind him, heavy footfalls signaled The Maniac's final approach. Though walking, he moved with an uncanny speed. Of course he did. He was no man; he was evil personified.

Harris said nothing as he towered over Murphy, who sunk to the ground, defeated. He had given up hope of escaping either monster, Glenwood Corrections, and The Maniac of D Block, so what use was it to fight? If he were lucky, his resignation would bring a swift death, rather than the untold agony Harris' earlier victims had faced.

Murphy thought of his wife. His son. She had been right all along. He'd been selfish in taking a man's life. It didn't matter that the scumbag had gotten off with a light sentence. He'd served his time, piece of shit or not. Murphy was neither judge, jury, nor executioner, but for one ill-fated moment in time, he fancied himself all three, and it had ruined the lives of his entire family. They'd continue to pay for his mistakes. Maybe in death, their debt would cease.

Murphy looked into Harris' mangled, rotting face. "Do it, you son of a bitch."

Harris said nothing. His massive chest rose and fell. It seemed even in death the body remembers such autonomic functions. Beside him, O'Rourke materialized.

"You tricked me," Murphy said.

O'Rourke shook his head. "I did no such thing. I gave you a map, nothing more, nothing less. I made no promises to you. We all make our own choices. *You* never seem to make the right one. Always looking to take things into your own hands rather than let them play out naturally. But no matter, we all leave Glenwood one way or another." O'Rourke winked out of existence as suddenly as he had appeared.

Out of the corner of his eye, Murphy saw the baton crashing downward. He felt a moment of impact—an intense pain in the top of his skull. The sharpened metal defense weapon pierced through his skull and skewered his brain, exiting from his chin with a gout of blood, skull fragments and brain matter exploding from the top of his skull and the newly formed hole in the soft skin behind his chin.

Murphy served his time, in Glenwood, and on earth. He'd finally reached the holy grail of the incarcerated—expiration of sentence.

AFTERWORD

I wrote this novella for a project which was released last year, called *The Conservator's Collection: Derelict*. Hot off my debut novella, which had gotten good reviews but had yet to pick up steam, and my collection which has also been well received, but has sold softly I attended author con 2 as a vendor.

The con was a large event, and my table ended up in a section outside of the main area alongside some other great authors, including Jay Bower. The area we were in received much less foot traffic, and it wasn't for lack of effort by the convention staff. Far from it. There was plenty of signage all over the place, but for whatever reason, people didn't seem to follow the signs. That ended up being a good thing, as it left me plenty of time to get to know Jay. We chatted quite a bit and exchanged phone numbers. The event came to a close and we made our own separate ways back home.

Life went on. I continued writing. In the indie horror scene you need to keep churning out work, especially if you aren't one of the bigger names. I don't make the rules, that's just the way it is. So I kept working on the next book and eventually I hit the 30k word mark. Around that time, I realized something terrifying. The unfinished manuscript was a steaming pile of crap. I was worried because I'd put so much time and effort into my second book length project and I *knew* that the entire thing needed to be written again from the ground up. I'd done it before. Those of you who've followed me at all probably know that's exactly what happened with *The Warrior Retreat*, but that doesn't make the task any less daunting, especially not when you'd already been worried about following up a well-received debut.

So I stopped writing. I procrastinated. I found any excuse to not work on the book. Until one day, about a month after author con, I got a text message from Jay asking if I wanted to work on a project with him. I said yes, although I was hesitant. Not because I didn't want to work with Jay, but because I was a fan of his work and I knew that my writing was at a standstill at the moment. My work in progress was atrocious, and I had no other ideas to pivot to. Jay pitched me a project with multiple authors contributing novelette length stories, an anthology of sorts. Something like *Tales From The Crypt*.

I loved the idea and said yes without really thinking about it. But we needed another author, so after about 10 seconds of deliberation, we both knew it had to be John Durgin. Lucky for us, John agreed right away and *The Conservator's Collection* was born.

But what about my lack of ideas? Well, that problem fixed itself shortly after Durgin signed on. No sooner than we settled on a theme, a fully formed idea popped into my brain. It demanded to be written. I always hate the pitch of *THIS X THAT*, but with *Expiration of Sentence*, my mind immediately screamed *Prison Break X Maniac Cop*.

The book wrote itself. I finished the first draft fairly quickly, especially considering the snail's pace I usually write. Once that was done, I took my sweet ass time on the subsequent drafts because I was worried about what the hell was I going to write after I'm done with this. I finished the book well ahead of deadline, if only so I wouldn't screw my co-authors. Our project was ready to go, and Bower and Durgin both knocked it out of the park with their respective entries. If you're reading this, and you haven't read the *The Conservator's Collection* and have no plans to, you really should grab their novellas, *Eyebiter's Revenge* by Jay Bower, and *Blank Space*, by John Durgin. I told him to subtitle it *Durgin's Version*. He did not.

The book you hold in your hand is something I wanted to release as a standalone as well. I'd discussed this with Bower and Durgin, and they were cool with it. Originally, that wasn't part of the plan, and if my book had stayed at the 15k word limit we had set for ourselves than I'd have left it where it was in *The Conservator's Collection* and moved on.

But the story demanded to be bigger, longer. I couldn't make it interesting without adding another 15k words to the limit. Lucky for me, Jay and John were on board not only with me doubling our agreed upon word limit, but they understood I was proud of the story and wanted to release it as a standalone book once our project had been out in the wild.

And that is why you're holding this book in your hands. Thank you for supporting my writing. I know this will be the second time some of you have bought this, not because I pulled the wool over your eyes, but because my readers are some of the most awesome, supportive people. Thank you all for taking this ride with me. If not for your support this wouldn't be possible. I promise to keep pushing forward. I hope you'll stay on this journey with me.

JL

ABOUT THE AUTHOR

John Lynch is a horror author from Rhode Island. He lives at home with his Wife, children, cat, and English Bulldog. He decided early on in his career that he would be known for using the term tube steak in every book that he writes. Please follow his author page on Facebook and other social media sites for the latest updates.

facebook.com/johnlynchbooks

x.com/johnlynchbooks

instagram.com/johnlynchbooks

bookbub.com/authors/john-lynch-2608700b-3091-4ba0-bedf-183bd0cd7cb1

goodreads.com/john_lynch

amazon.com/author/johnlynchbooks

tiktok.com/@johnlynchhorror

ALSO BY JOHN LYNCH

The Warrior Retreat

Christmas Eve Carnage

Woe To Those Who Dwell on Earth

www.ingramcontent.com/pod-product-compliance
Lightning Source LLC
Chambersburg PA
CBHW030148010826
48973CB00002B/783